Contents

A Reason to Kill

Steve Higgs

The Phone Call

I was queuing to buy a hotdog from a street stand when my phone rang. The sound of it made my right eye twitch for there was no good reason for anyone to be calling me; not so far as I could see.

In New York for a two-day break with my boyfriend, Alistair, I wanted to be left alone by pretty much everyone else on the planet. I wanted to do daft touristy stuff like eat a hotdog in the street with the backdrop of Times Square all around me. It was just after noon on our first day and so far I hadn't really been anywhere or done anything.

Savouring the sights and sounds, there were people everywhere I looked - it truly is a bustling metropolis, and they were all going places. The smell of car exhaust fumes mixed with the odour of food and a cold breeze bit at my face each time the wind blew.

I'd chosen to dress for the occasion. A new camel-coloured winter coat fell almost to my knees where it met the top of a pair of brand-new brown boots that hugged my calves. The boots matched the shade of leather on my handbag, which I carried looped over my right arm. I wore a dress for once which is something I typically avoid because my working life requires me to run all too often.

I might be running to chase someone – I'm employed as a detective on board a cruise ship. Equally, I might be running to get away as the people I chase sometimes want me to stop trying to catch them committing whatever heinous or ridiculous crime they might have

1

chosen to pursue. Truthfully, I get a lot of the latter. Thankfully, I have a team of armed security officers to assist me, and they can generally be relied upon to intervene before I get killed.

Then there is my butler, Jermaine. When I first boarded the cruise ship, I found myself staying in the royal suite which comes with a member of staff, a bit like Downton Abbey. I mention the famous British period drama because Jermaine is Jamaican, but speaks as though he is among the cast of the show. He doesn't like to admit it, but the accent is one hundred percent fake, perfected over many hours as he watched the episodes on loop.

Jermaine is my dearest friend and my protector. He wasn't by my side for once which was entirely due to me wanting to spend the day with Alistair.

Unfortunately, we had not got off to the best start, getting delayed by many hours when Alistair got caught up dealing with a small matter that demanded his attention. As the captain of a cruise ship, it was one of the inevitabilities of his post.

My name is Patricia Fisher. I'm a fifty-three-year-old woman from England. I have an ex-husband, no kids, and a life story that could be turned into a book if I thought anyone would believe it. I live and work on the Aurelia, a giant floating city of a cruise ship that is currently docked in the famous American city.

When Gloria's voice filled my ear, I found myself pulling the phone away from my head to check the screen – it didn't display her number as it ought to if she were calling and the number wasn't hers.

Not that I can recall her number, but there are definitely a pair of fours in it somewhere. This number had an odd prefix, and it took me a moment to realise that the call had been placed locally from a pay phone.

Do those even exist anymore?

My confusion deepening, I put the phone back to my ear. "I'm sorry, Gloria, can you say all that again."

Gloria is a passenger aboard the cruise ship, but also a paid member of the crew despite being in her eighties. She came by the role due to my insistence that my assistant, Sam Chalk, was taken on when I was given the job of ship's detective. Still with me? Sorry if this is getting complicated. Sam has Downs Syndrome, or as Americans prefer to call it, Down Syndrome. Whichever way you want to say it, Sam was born with cognitive limitations, but not ones that stop him from doing much.

He became my assistant when I briefly ran my own detective agency in England, and came to the ship with me when we were all forced to flee a crazy gang boss called The Godmother. She's in jail now, by the way. Sam needed someone to live with him just to make sure his uniform gets ironed and he remembers to shave and turn up for work – he can be easily distracted and that's where his paternal grandmother, Gloria, comes in.

That's the short version, believe it or not, and the reason you need to know all that is because Gloria is a bigger handful than her grandson. Unlike the stereotypical grandmother I envisage in my head, Gloria can be trouble in capital letters and will deliberately do things she has been advised not to, just to see what might happen.

"We saw a man get murdered," Gloria repeated.

I really hadn't been paying attention because I thought she said she'd been arrested.

"And we got arrested when we attempted to force our way into a building to apprehend the killer before he could escape."

Oh, super. So I did hear correctly.

The hot dog queue moved forward and the man behind the street cart aimed an eyebrow in my direction.

"What'll it be?" he asked.

I held up a hand to apologise and stepped away, letting the person behind me fill the gap. My stomach rumbled as though it were protesting my decision to deal with what felt like a more pressing issue than my lunch.

3

Alistair was a few feet away, talking on his phone to his chief of engineering, Commander Philips. Commander Philips and I do not see eye to eye, but have managed to achieve a truce of sorts by simply avoiding one another.

I tugged at Alistair's sleeve while talking to Gloria and when he turned my way, I covered the mouthpiece of my phone to say, "Gloria's been arrested along with two of her friends."

I feel it speaks volumes about my life that his reply was, "Of course she has." Wrapping up his call with an insistent, "Deal with it. I expect to leave on time tomorrow," Alistair hung up.

I was getting confusing details from Sam's gran; she told a story by starting in the middle and jumping about from pertinent point to pertinent point as they occurred to her. To get a clearer picture, I would need to sit her down and make her go through it slowly.

"Gloria!" I tried to cut over the top of her. "Gloria!" She kept right on talking. "GLO-RIA!"

"Yes, dear?"

"Just tell me where you are. I will come to you."

"Only if it's convenient, Patricia," she replied, her voice filled with fake apology.

I will admit a temporary temptation to reply that it wasn't convenient right now and that I could swing by tomorrow. Days when it is just me and my beau are few and far between and I had hoped this two day break in New York would pass uninterrupted. No such luck.

Dismissing the temptingly evil voice in my head, I promised to be there within the hour.

Coming off the phone, I muttered to myself, "Thirty-seventh precinct. Why does that sound familiar?" I discovered the answer thirty-two minutes later when the cab pulled up outside a building I knew.

This was my second time in New York and I got to see none of it the first time because I was trying to help a friend whose brother had been arrested for murder. The one place I did see was the thirty-seventh precinct police station where the brother in question was being held.

Now I was back here, and though I wasn't happy about it, since I had no choice in the matter, I could at least walk into the place knowing one person who worked there.

Alistair paid the cab fare with a tap of his card and held the door for me to get out.

On the way over, he'd quizzed me for more detail, wanting to know what Gloria and friends had seen and why they were now in custody.

I didn't have a lot of detail to give, but told him what I knew.

"They were sightseeing on one of those open-top buses, taking in the sights and sounds of the city." Such trips were offered by the cruise ship in conjunction with the companies operating them and were very popular with the less physically capable passengers of which we always had plenty. "Gloria told me they were halfway through when the bus stopped at a junction and they saw a man strangling another man with a length of rope in the adjacent building. According to Gloria it was at the exact same level as the top deck they were sitting on. She tried to get the bus to stop, but the driver refused until Gloria and her friends kicked up enough that the tour operator decided it was safer to just kick them off."

Alistair frowned. "How did that result in them getting arrested?"

In the back of the cab I had sighed and rubbed my forehead. "That bit didn't. It was what came after that. The ladies backtracked to the building – an office block of businesses in the heart of Manhattan's financial district. There they harangued the lady on reception. She wouldn't let them in and told them to call the cops."

"They hadn't called the cops at that point?"

"Apparently not." The truth was Gloria hadn't called the cops because of me. I solve crimes every week and she fancied having a go herself. Pushing on, I said, "Gloria chose to create a diversion, getting one of her friends to knock over the water cooler."

"How did she manage that?" Alistair asked, incredulous.

I sighed again. "She rammed it with her scooter." Gloria got a mobility scooter a while back – another thing I could be blamed for since I bought it. With it she joined the horde of pension-aged passengers who zip around the Aurelia's decks on four tiny wheels. In general terms, the mobility devices were of enormous benefit, and I wondered how older, less able people used to get around. Gloria, however, was a menace on hers and a terrible influence on those she made friends with.

"Let me guess," said Alistair. "While the lady on reception tried to deal with the mess, Gloria's Gang buzzed themselves into the building and went looking for their killer."

"Or the murder scene," I offered. "I got a little confused myself at that point. Gloria is not one for telling stories in a linear fashion. Anyway, the receptionist called the cops, and they showed up before Gloria's Gang," I decided that was a catchy term for them and used it myself, "could find what they were looking for. I'm guessing the cops arrested them just to shut them up."

Strictly speaking, dealing with arrested passengers ashore fell outside of my remit. Were it not Sam's grandmother, I wouldn't be getting involved, but standing in front of the police station, I found myself filled with a dreaded sense that my entire New York break was about to go out the window.

Don't you just hate when your worst premonitions turn out to be a mile short of how bad it is about to be?

A Familiar Face

The precinct building – honestly, I'm not sure what the locals call it, but to me it's a police station and I know that's thoroughly English – was what one might call 'a little run down'. The façade was stained with age and the same graffiti I saw last time was still visible though more had been added.

Frankly, I marvelled that someone would think to daub a police station. How did they get away with it? Was it just that the police has far bigger issues to deal with so let kids with spray cans get away with such misdemeanours?

I pushed through the door to find myself in the familiar reception area. To my left, hard plastic chairs were bolted to the floor and dead ahead, a built-in hatch with a protective screen – you don't see those in England – housed a pair of cops in uniform. The man and woman were in their late thirties and both carried a goodly amount of pounds around their midriff or, in the woman's case, hips, that probably hadn't been there a decade ago.

The woman wore three stripes on her arm – a sergeant, unless I had that completely wrong. I was on my way to her, and her head was just rising to look at me when the very person I hoped to see came through the door behind her.

"Lieutenant Danvers!" I called to get his attention, the words bursting from my mouth the moment I saw his face. He looked just as tired and harassed as last time I was here.

Twitching at the sound of his name, he took one look at me and dropped his eyes away again. I saw his mouth form an expletive and he seemed to slump before my eyes, his shoulders drooping and his head hanging so low his chin was almost on his chest.

The sergeant turned toward him. "You know this lady, Captain?"

Captain? He'd been promoted.

Danvers, whatever rank he now held, raised his head again and looking as though he carried the weight of the world on his shoulders, he said, "You're here about the old ladies, aren't you? You were the phone call, right?"

Smiling pleasantly, for what else was I supposed to do, I nodded my head. "That's right. Are they free to go?"

Danvers muttered something under his breath before shaking his head and staring at the ceiling like he was offering up a prayer.

Two minutes later I was in his office. Alistair was in the chair next to mine and Captain Danvers – his name was stencilled on the door – was slumped in the chair behind the desk.

"Are you related to any of the crazy old ladies I have in my lock up?"

I shook my head. "Not exactly. Gloria is the grandmother of my assistant."

Danvers muttered something I didn't catch and sat up straighter in his chair.

"You know what? I don't care. You can have them."

"There's no bail to pay?" Alistair sought to confirm, his forehead wrinkling.

"If there were, I would pay it for you," Danvers joked. Probably joked. How much trouble had they been? "They're not being charged with anything and the damage they did was minimal. None of that concerns me."

"What does?" I enquired, keen to get to the point. Maybe if we could get Gloria's Gang out of here quickly enough, Alistair and I could go back to our day.

Captain Danvers fixed me with a hard stare. "Frankly, Mrs Fisher, your presence in New York concerns me. Last time you were here I got shot."

I winced at the memory.

"Last time you were here, three rival gangs faced off against each other in what could have easily ended in a total bloodbath. If you came in on the same ship as the old ladies currently in my lockup ..." he looked for me to confirm that was the case, "then you have been here less than a day and already I find you in trouble."

"How am I in trouble?" I felt he was being rather unfair, and it wasn't as though I shot him during my last visit.

I got a grimace this time as he muttered, "That's what I'm waiting to find out." Before I could raise an objection, he said, "I'm releasing the old dears into your care. I don't want any more of this 'witnessed a murder' nonsense, and I don't expect to hear your name again, Mrs Fisher. Are we clear?"

I could have said, 'Perfectly clear', I'm sure that was what he wanted, but I didn't. It's not a defiant streak running through me, but a need to let the world know Patricia Fisher is not about to be pushed around. I had done nothing wrong. Not on this occasion or the last, and since he chose to bring the murder subject up, I felt inclined to pursue it.

"What did they witness?" I asked.

Captain Danvers' eyebrows did a little dance. He wasn't expecting to answer questions.

"They didn't see anything," he stated flatly. "My officers searched the building after the ladies were escorted outside and taken away. They found nothing. No sign of a struggle, no dead body, and surprisingly enough, no killer."

I pursed my lips and skewed them to one side while I considered his response. Until this point it had been my assumption that Gloria *had* seen a murder. She was wilful, defiant, obstinate, and possessed a tendency to ignore rules. She was not, however, given to flights of fantasy.

However, seeing no reason to question him further, I gathered my handbag, and began to rise.

"Thank you for your time, Captain Danvers. Congratulations on your promotion."

He made a scoffing noise, "Pffft. Promotion? Being the captain here is more like a death sentence. The last three guys all retired after heart attacks in their fifties. I can feel my blood pressure rising by the day." To accentuate his point, Danvers pulled a small plastic container from his pocket – the kind you get from the pharmacy - shook two pills into his hand and downed them without a drink. "I should quit, that's what I should do. Got any vacancies on that cruise ship of yours?"

My eyebrows showed my surprise and I was turning to Alistair when Danvers spoke again.

"That was a joke, Mrs Fisher. I hate the ocean almost as much as I hate my ex-wives." He came around his desk, heading for the door. "Wait in reception. I'll have the old dears brought out to you."

Done talking, he hung out of his office door to whistle for a uniformed officer who would escort us back to where we came in only to come face to face with a gruff looking man ten years his senior. He had beady eyes and a sweaty forehead. He stank like cigarettes, and I could see where decades of smoking had ruined his skin and teeth. Somewhere close to sixty, he had tidy grey hair with just a few speckles of black in the lower extremities of his sideburns and glasses with a thick black frame.,

"This is the woman?" he questioned, eyeing me with suspicion while rudely referring to me without introducing himself.

"Yes, sir," Captain Danvers replied wearily.

Whoever the man was, he was the captain's boss. What rank did that make him? He was in a suit, so I had no way of telling.

Contemptuous eyes still aimed my way, the man said, "I hope you read her the riot act."

Unhappy at being spoken about, I chose to answer for myself. "Why would he need to do that? Who are you and why is it that you believe I should be spoken to with anything other than polite respect?"

The man made a scoffing noise. "I am the chief of police, thank you very much, Mrs Fisher. This is my city to protect and the best way to do that, in light of your previous visit, is to send you back to your cruise ship and keep you there."

Alistair didn't like that one bit. "The chief of police? I rather think the mayor would like to discuss your policy regarding the passengers and crew of my cruise ship."

"Your cruise ship?" the scoffing continued. "You're nothing but the captain of it, *Mister* Huntley." The chief made very sure to ignore Alistair's rank. "And we are not talking about the passengers and crew, just one of them."

Turning to Captain Danvers and effectively dismissing us, he spat, "See to it that she leaves New York and does not return. Oh, and get those old bags out of my lockup. I want you back on the Columbian problem, Captain Danvers. No excuses. I want results!" Spinning on his heel, the chief of police strode away without feeling the need to have his instructions discussed.

Captain Danvers rubbed at his chest, clearly in some discomfort.

"Are you okay?" I asked.

My question made him react as though it were a slap to his face.

"I'm fine! The chief is right: you are trouble. You're going to tell me I don't have the authority to send you back to your ship and that is one hundred percent correct. I do, however, have the authority to arrest you. I can keep you in a cell until your ship is due to leave. I beg that you do not give me a reason to do so."

Now whyever would I do that?

Pointing which way we should go, Captain Danvers set off in the other direction.

Choosing to stand when we reached the reception area – it's not like the plastic chairs were comfortable to sit on – I nestled in close to Alistair and said, "You were quiet." It's not that I needed him to have my back or be vocally on my side against Danvers, I was more than capable of handling his bluster. However, Alistair let it all pass by without comment.

He grinned down at me. "A man should know when to let the woman talk, my dear. And what would I have said? They called you about a crime; this is the Patricia Fisher show. If they wanted to charge the ladies or in some way impede their return to the ship, I would have of course expressed my deepest reservations. That not being the case, I feel the police have acted as they ought."

I hate when he makes perfect sense. Why does he have to be so logical and rational all the time?

"Besides," he continued. "Do you really think Gloria Chalk and her friends are going to let this go? They'll want to rope you into helping them solve the case whether they saw something or imagined it."

Further discussion of the matter proved impossible for Gloria's Gang were approaching.

"I don't need to be helped, young man. I'm not an invalid," protested Pearl. I should have guessed Gloria would be with Pearl and Peggy. The twin sisters are two ladies from a rolling group Gloria spends her spare time with. Passengers come and go all the time, the length of their stay on board dictated by their desires and their budget. These two were relative newcomers, but Gloria had fallen in tight with them. I could not remember where they were from – somewhere in one of the northern US states, I believed, but I could recall they both worked for the IRS for many, many years and that, upon learning this, most American passengers chose to give them a wide birth.

"Just return our scooters and we'll be on our way," complained Peggy. "I still don't see why you felt the need to take them away in the first place."

The door leading behind reception opened, the face of a harassed-looking young man in uniform holding it open to let the ladies through. Another cop followed behind them, probably to make sure they left. He was only about six feet tall, but that made him half a foot taller than the ladies who were all on the short side and undoubtedly a couple of inches shorter than they were in their twenties.

Gloria led the way, storming into the reception area as fast as she could go on two feet and a walking stick. Her face was set to thunderous, her scowl such that it would melt the pattern from a China plate.

"Wait here, please," requested the cop holding the door. "Your scooters will be brought out shortly."

Gloria didn't bother to respond; she'd seen me and was making a beeline across the reception area.

"Patricia, thank goodness," she started talking before she was halfway to me. "These idiots couldn't solve a murder if the killer waited around with the body to give a confession. With your help we'll have it sewn up by sundown." Still on her way across the reception area – she wasn't fast on her feet – she stopped and shuffled around to address her friends. "I told you Patricia was the right person to call. We're out already and the real investigation can begin."

Peggy 'accidentally' whacked the young man holding the door on the shin with her walking stick as she passed.

"Oh, goodness," she mock gasped. "I'm so sorry. You must forgive me. I'm getting so wobbly on my feet these days."

The cop winced and refused to rub his leg lest his colleagues tease him. I thought for a moment she was going to give him another whack for good measure, but distracted by Gloria, who was still talking, Peggy ambled along to join her party.

Peggy and Pearl are eighty-something-year-old twins who never married and have lived together since their parents passed and left them the house more than six decades ago. They both wore their pure white hair with a tight perm that kept it neat and close to their heads. They dressed similarly too, opting for cotton trousers, sturdy boots and long coats to ward off the early winter temperatures.

In fact, the only way I could tell them apart was due to the fact that Pearl always wore pearl earrings and her sister, Peggy, did not.

Not wanting to raise my voice, even though Gloria's Gang were happy to do so, I waited until Gloria was close enough to hear me when I spoke at a low volume.

"Gloria, we are not going to investigate. Captain Danvers said his officers searched the building and couldn't find any sign of a struggle, let alone a murder."

"Ha!" she spat. "That fool couldn't find his bottom with both hands in his back pockets."

"Shhh!" I tried to hush her.

It had the opposite effect. She turned around to yell at the sergeant behind the reception desk.

"Telling me what I saw? There was a murder! Blind idiots the lot of you!"

The woman in the sergeant's uniform cocked an eyebrow and murmured something to her colleague though her eyes never left our group.

"We need to leave," I insisted, attempting to steer the ladies to the exit.

"We need our scooters," Pearl reminded me.

Gloria, now mercifully bored of berating the police officers, turned her thoughts back to the supposed murder. "And his officers didn't search the building, not unless you think that can be done in less than five minutes. They might have looked through a few windows, but they didn't have time to do more than that."

The door by reception opened again, a different young man in uniform wheeling a mobility scooter through it. There were two more behind him, and moments later the scooter brigade were mounted up and ready to go.

"Where to first then, Patricia?" Gloria wanted to know the moment we were on the street in front of the station. "Back to the scene of the crime, yes?"

"No!" I realised my voice had come out a little harsh and toned it down when I repeated, "No, Gloria. I have no jurisdiction here. I'm not saying you didn't see anything, but we can't just go snooping around where we have no right to be. You were arrested once today already. Don't you think going back to the same building will end the same way? The lady working there won't be pleased to see you."

Speaking as though she hadn't listened to a word I said, Pearl remarked, "Yeah, she needs to answer some questions too. Pretending like she didn't know what was going on. She asked us which firm we were there to visit when we first entered the building. She must do the same to everyone, so how would she not know who was in the first floor office at the front?"

"She was covering up for someone," agreed Peggy.

"Ladies," Alistair finally decided to get involved. "It seems ill-advised to go against Mrs Fisher's advice."

I tugged his arm, turning him to face me so I could hiss quietly, "That's it? Can't you do something to stop them? You're the captain of the ship, for goodness sake."

I got a bemused look from him. "I'm only their captain when I am on the ship, Patricia, and then it's not as though they are my subordinates. I am a glorified tour guide, darling. My purpose is to ensure they get to where they are going and have the most fabulous time doing it. On land I have no purpose at all."

Okay, so I knew that was all true, but I still believed he could insist they see reason.

My phone rang, the sound coming from my handbag to interrupt my train of thought. All three old ladies were looking my way, expecting me to say something about their case, and I answered the phone to escape their gazes.

The screen displayed the name 'Barbie'. Barbara 'Barbie' Berkeley is one of my friends from the ship. She's a twenty-two-year-old Californian blonde gym instructor with a gravity defying chest and a face and figure that could grace a magazine cover or a Hollywood red carpet.

She sounded upbeat when she spoke – situation normal for her.

"Patty! Guess what I found?"

That provided me with a broad gamut of options.

"Do I get a hint?"

She laughed in my ear. "I'm at the museum, silly. Don't you remember the conversation this morning?"

Oh, yes. The small matter of the murdered stowaway and the fortune in treasure he carried. How Finn Murphy came to be on board the Aurelia and below deck with a knife sticking out of his chest was a mystery I was yet to solve. It was sufficient to keep me awake at night – I don't like unresolved cases.

The murder was just the tip of the iceberg though his autopsy revealed a small fortune in uncut gems in his gut and when we found his tatty, grubby sleeping bag and battered backpack, it was full to the brim with coins worth far more than their weight in gold. On top of that haul he had jewel encrusted items of jewellery and more. Millions of dollars' worth in the possession of a man who looked to be starving to death.

Even that paled into comparison with the enigma that followed. News of the murder and the gems became public knowledge, the inevitable attention drawing a professor of maritime antiquities to seek me out.

Introducing himself as Professor Noriega, it transpired that he was a phoney and most likely the person responsible for killing the real Professor Noriega in Rio de Janeiro. The haul of treasure was stolen from my cabin by a second man, a giant who fought off Alistair and then my butler who, let me assure you, has never been beaten in a fight since I met him.

Following the trail to Rio, we discovered the treasure was almost certainly from a Spanish ship called the San José. Records showed it sank off the coast of Columbia more than three hundred years ago, but little snippets of research and the fake Professor Noriega's murderous interest in it was sufficient to make me believe the treasure was somewhere other than the bottom of the ocean.

Quite where it could be, or how it was that the history books had it wrong, was yet another intriguing facet of the mystery.

Barbie, despite looking like a Barbie doll, had a brain the size of a walrus's bottom and was a whizz at finding information on the internet. For weeks she had been piecing together little clues about the ship and digging into historic archives where they were accessible online. There were thousands of hits for the San José, which she had to then pick through to find those with merit.

This morning she told me she was going to visit the museum here in New York. I forget the name of it now, but it has a maritime history section and lists items from the San José among its artefacts.

Unable to guess what Barbie might have discovered, I begged that she tell me.

"There's a series of letters, Patty. Written by one of the officers, Lieutenant Bernadino Alvarez. They are to his sweetheart, begging her to join him in England. He apologises that he cannot ever return to Spain, though he never says why, and laments that he has little to offer her. It's really quite sad, Patty."

Gloria's Gang were colluding again, and half my attention was on them, my ears pricked to hear what they were saying. My focus was further divided by Alistair who was on the phone again with Commander Philips and clearly not happy; his body language told me everything.

Wading through my fog of confusion, I asked, "Sorry, Barbie, you were saying something about some letters. Why are they pertinent?"

"Because he's one of the officers aboard the San José, Patty. He died in England more than forty years after the ship supposedly sank on the other side of the Atlantic."

The back of my skull itched.

"Sooo, you're saying that's proof the ship didn't sink, right."

"Well, it's proof of something. I'm still going through the letters and other artefacts. He couldn't return to his sweetheart in Spain and I think that was because he was supposed to be dead. If they faked the San José sinking, how would he explain his sudden reappearance?"

"Yes, but then where is the ship and all its treasure?" I felt I made a valid point and we had been going around and around about this simple question as a team since the very start. If it hadn't gone to the bottom of the ocean, then where was it? How do you hide a Spanish treasure galleon for three hundred years?

"That remains a question to be answered, but it's not just Lieutenant Alvarez. You already know about the other artefacts ... there's too many clues to ignore. The ship is out there somewhere, Patty. Or the treasure is. Are you coming to the museum?"

I told her I would if there was anything worth looking at. She was there with Deepa Bhukari and Martin Baker, two more security officers from my team, and her boyfriend Dr Hideki Nakamura, the junior doctor aboard the ship. They were among a very small group who knew about Finn Murphy's treasure. Alistair was another and though we had plans for our time in New York, we both agreed to join them if the team found something worthwhile.

I glanced at Alistair. His free hand was gesticulating wildly. He kept his voice low so no one would hear what was being said, but it was clear things were not going according to plan. He was yet to share with me the nature of this particular drama, but if I was to place a bet, it would be that he was about to announce he needed to return to the ship.

Gloria's Gang were still in a huddle, whispering back and forth.

"Patty? Are you there?" Barbie's voice in my ear brought me back to the present.

"Yes, sorry. I'll ... I'll be there shortly, okay. I've got a couple of things to take care of first." I thanked her and reiterated my promise to get there as soon as I could. I didn't like that they were spending their precious shore time working on a case, but with the exception of Hideki, who is a Japanese native and in New York for the first time in his life, the rest had visited the city many times, that being the nature of life aboard a cruise ship. Also, they were not only volunteers, but had insisted this was what they wanted to do.

With Alistair still on his call, I dropped my phone back into its pouch inside my handbag and went to Gloria. Touching her shoulder to break up the old ladies' little conflab, I made sure they were listening before I started to speak.

"Ladies, it concerns me greatly that you want to pursue this case. What do you hope to gain?"

Peggy was the first to respond, snorting her thoughts derisively.

"You were right, Gloria. She does think she's the only one who can solve a mystery."

"Wait, that's not ..."

"She's probably going to tell us we should head back to the ship," remarked Pearl, folding her arms over her deflated chest as she defied me to say that wasn't the case.

"Well, I think ..."

"Come on, Patricia," begged Gloria, cutting into the conversation as the one on my side. "What harm can it do? We know what we saw. It was right in front of our faces. The biggest mystery is that no one else on the bus saw it."

Peggy said, "They were all gawping at the Empire State building. Like that's as interesting as seeing someone get strangled." Peggy had a worrying amount of glee in her eyes as she recalled the images from her memory.

I knew I was being pushed into a corner, manipulated by three old ladies who would prey on my conscience and ego if they thought it would work.

Taking a steadying breath, I said, "Explain it all again, please, starting at the top."

When they finished, it wasn't their words that convinced me, but the conviction with which they said them. All three ladies stuck to the same story, but now in a manner that suggested it had not been rehearsed. They all remembered the incident in a slightly different way, but the details they gave reinforced and corroborated the individual versions rather than giving me reason to dispute what I heard.

My conclusion: they *had* seen something.

It wasn't on the cruise ship, and I could easily refuse to get involved. I'll admit there was a voice in my head yelling at me to walk away. However, Gloria's Gang were not about to stop their dogged pursuit of the truth and I figured it was easier to join in until their curiosity had been satisfied than to collect them from custody again in a few hours' time.

"Okay," I relented. "Let's go take a look."

I turned to find Alistair's call was at an end. His muscles were tense, a sure sign he was battling rising anger.

Facing me, his features softened, and I knew he was going to apologise. Sure enough, he needed to return to the ship. There was something broken that could not easily be fixed. He didn't want to tell me about it now, and said he would know more in a few hours.

He looked genuinely and quite thoroughly hacked off that our day was to be ruined, but there was nothing either one of us could do about it. There wasn't even any point in going with him because he would need to work.

We kissed on the street and I watched him hail a cab.

Keeping Secrets

- -

B arbie looked up when a shadow fell over her. To her left, a pile of photocopied letters bore highlighted marks and red rings around certain words. To her right sat an electronic notepad with a growing list of thoughts, notes, ideas, and questions. Directly below her head, a large tome had been holding her attention for the last thirty minutes.

"Good afternoon," said the man now staring down at her. He extended his hand when she met his eyes. "My name is Hugo Lockhart. I'm the assistant curator for maritime antiquities. I was told you have particular interest in the San José."

Barbie rose to her feet. Her boyfriend, Hideki, leaned out from behind a bookshelf where he had been inspecting another hefty book that listed all Spanish naval activity in the period preceding 1708, when the San José was reported as sunk in battle, and the next few years that followed. It seemed improbable, if not impossible that a huge Spanish treasure ship could have sailed away without the world finding out, but that was the theory the team were currently exploring.

Deepa Bhukari and her husband, Martin Baker, were sitting a few yards away amidst a pile of books at another table. They looked up to listen when the assistant curator started speaking.

"That's right," said Barbie, shaking the man's hand. He had a soft grip which she hadn't expected, forcing her to adjust the crushing vice she intended to employ as their hands met. "I'm Barbara Berkeley. Is that something you can help with?"

Hugo nodded and met the group with an engaging smile. "It is my primary purpose, Miss Berkeley."

"Oh, call me Barbie, please."

Hugo nodded again, doing his best not to notice the blonde woman's ample chest and toned body. She was utterly delicious and her friend with the darker skin was no slouch in the looks department either. Making a mental note to sort out his dating life – he'd clearly been single for way too long – Hugo got down to business.

"I see one of my associates was good enough to provide you with one of our most recent discoveries."

"You mean the letters Bernadino Alvarez wrote," Barbie touched the pile of photocopies; they were not going to let people anywhere near the real ones.

Hugo's smile turned wistful. "Yes. I'm afraid our initial research suggests they might be fakes. Either that or part of an elaborate fantasy Senor Alvarez chose to invent."

Barbie frowned. That didn't sound right at all.

Sensing that she was about to start arguing, Hugo got in first.

"You are no doubt investigating the possibility that the San José was not, in fact, sunk as reported in 1708, and was instead taken in secret to a location that is yet to be discovered, the treasure still secure in its hold." He paused to see if they would deny that was their intent, and continued. "There are many theories regarding the San José, some," he chuckled, "more fanciful than others, but all quite misleading."

Deepa crossed the room to join Barbie, followed by Martin and finally Hideki who still held the book he'd been inspecting.

"You're saying it did sink in 1708?" Deepa sought to confirm.

"Precisely. In an action with the British Royal Navy, the San José's armoury was breeched causing an explosion that tore the ship apart. It was all documented by the captain of the ship that fired the shot and by other ships in the battle. They intended to board her and take the treasure for England. Bad luck or poor judgement denied them their prize."

"How then do you explain these letters?" asked Martin, jabbing a finger at the photo-copies.

Deepa whispered, "He said they are most likely fakes, darling."

"Oh, yeah, he did say that," Martin muttered.

Barbie wasn't so easily dismissed.

"Multiple artefacts from the San José have been found in the years since it sank." Turning away from the assistant curator, she scrambled through the books and sheets on her desk to find the one she wanted. "Here," she showed Hugo a page with a photograph of an ornate chalice. "This was found not far from Southampton in England, the same country Lieutenant Alvarez chose to live out the rest of his life." She rummaged again. "These plates are part of a dinner service that was loaded aboard the San José as part of the Consuelos family's belongings. They travelled with the treasure ship so how was the dinner service found in Spain in 1937 if it went down with the ship in 1708?"

Hugo offered an apologetic smile. "I suspect the plates were stolen by a miscreant at the Port in the hours or days before the ship set sail. The items would have been reported missing only when the ship made port in Spain and their absence could be identified. Perhaps the thief only had time to get the plates and that's why only those were discovered. Just as likely is that the thief stole the whole dinner service, but in the years that followed the delicate porcelain was broken and the parts of the dinner service separated. Of course, the remainder could still be out there, tucked in the corner of a basement somewhere in the world. I doubt we will ever know."

"What about the chalice?" Deepa pressed. "It made it all the way to England. And what about Lieutenant Alvarez? He should have died along with the rest of the crew, yet he survived to live out his life in England."

"But did he?" asked Hugo. With quizzical expressions on the faces looking his way, he said, "We are still investigating the validity of the letters, but the most likely theory at this time is that the man who wrote the letters was a wanted criminal or someone who had reason to want to change his identity. He knew Bernadino Alvarez somehow and chose to assume his identity when he heard news of the ship's sinking. The letters would be part of the ruse to convince those around him he was who he said he was. The claim that he could not return to Spain might have been genuine though I suspect he arranged to have the replies written."

Barbie pressed her lips together. The assistant curator gave logical, rational responses, yet she also knew he was wrong. She just couldn't tell him how she could be so certain. Finn Murphy found the treasure, that they knew for certain. It was their secret though and it was going to stay that way.

"Thank you," Barbie dipped her head in thanks. "If it's all right with you, we will continue researching. Everything you say makes sense, but what if you are wrong?"

"If I am wrong? Well then, the San José and billions in treasure are still out there somewhere waiting to be found. Good luck to you, Barbie," he met the eyes of the three people standing to her left and right, "and to all of you. I fear your endeavours will follow in the footsteps of the many scholars and treasure hunters who have likewise tried to find this particular fortune."

Hugo retreated, checking over his shoulder just once when he reached the door. They were all back at it, their heads in books as they looked for the one thing that might get them a step closer to the treasure. For his part, Hugo held no belief the San José had gone anywhere other than to the bottom of the ocean, but he kept a special interest in it because he was paid to.

Closing the door behind him, he quickened his pace. He needed to make a phone call and was about as keen to do so as he had ever been.

For seven years he'd kept a phone number on a business card in his wallet. There was nothing else on the business card, just the number. A number he was to call if ever anyone showed particular interest in the San José.

He'd never met the man he was about to call, but remembered speaking to him most distinctly. Hugo received a monthly retainer directly into his bank for the promise he would dial the number when and if the time ever came to do so. Upon doing so, if the alert he gave proved to be accurate and worthy, the man he called would pay a sum that Hugo struggled to believe could be real.

One thing he knew for sure: he was going to place the call and keep his fingers crossed.

Taking his phone from his desk – they weren't supposed to carry them when they were working – Hugo walked to the nearest exit and stepped outside.

Feeling nervous, his hands clammy and his heartbeat fast, Hugo found himself looking over his shoulder and all around to make sure there was no one within earshot.

With a trembling finger, he copied the number from the creased and faded card into his phone and held it to his ear.

Across the Atlantic Ocean, Xavier Silvestre heard his phone ringing.

Houston Investments

"Whoa, there, ladies," I had to block Gloria, Peggy, and Pearl's advance with my body. "You're not going in."

We were standing outside a multi-storey edifice labelled, 'The Roosevelt Building'. In the heart of Manhattan's financial district, it housed several hedge fund and investment firms among other businesses.

"What?" Peggy's expression suggested she took my remark as a verbal slap. Pearl and Gloria clearly agreed.

"That lady at the reception desk knows you, right?" I asked a rhetorical question. "What do you think she is going to do the moment you step foot inside the building?"

"Oh," Gloria acknowledged that I had a point. "Yeah, I guess you're probably right."

"Let's tie her up then," suggested Pearl.

I checked to see if she was being serious. She was.

"You can distract her, Patricia," Peggy joined in. "And we'll ..."

"NO!" I left no doubt regarding my thoughts on the subject of tying people up.

"But she's clearly in on it, Patricia," argued Pearl. "I don't believe her story about the office being empty for one minute." We had gone over this several times. When they first burst into the Roosevelt Building, yelling at the lady working behind the reception desk that someone was being murdered upstairs, she strenuously assured them the office in question was empty.

"And you may be right," I chose to be diplomatic since disputing their claims only made them argue harder. "But for now, I want to keep her on the playing field, so to speak." I pointed across the street. "There is a coffee shop across the road. You can watch from over there."

"Ooh, I bet they have doughnuts," Gloria clapped her hands together. "And New York style cheesecake."

"Is that the kind they bake in the oven?" asked Peggy.

The ladies suitably distracted by food, I busied myself looking up the list of firms with offices inside the building. Once they were across the street and into the coffee shop, I made a call.

I like to think of myself as an honest person by which I mean that I never knowingly lie unless it is absolutely necessary. Right now it wasn't, but I doubted being truthful would work in my favour. Opting to label my intended actions as a ruse, rather than outright lies, I dialled the number on the website and waited for the call to connect.

"Good afternoon," a soft, but identifiable, Brooklyn accent invaded my ear. "Global Investment Syndicate. To whom may I direct your call?"

"Brett Flowers, please. This is Gaynor Goodman," I made the name up on the spot, "calling on behalf of John Oswald of Oswald Enterprises." The name might mean something to the woman answering the call or it might not. The hedge fund manager I asked to speak to though; well, I was willing to bet he would know the name of one of America's richest men. Especially since John Oswald was a headline news story only yesterday when two of his ex-wives were murdered.

"One moment, please."

The line switched to music, the kind you listen to in an elevator, before the woman's voice returned.

"Connecting you now."

Convincing Brett Flowers, one of the lower tier investors they had working at the firm (according to their website), to meet me right now, was even easier than I expected. My explanation that I was in town for a meeting that had been cancelled and hoped to fill my time with something proactive needed only the slightest nudge to get it over the line. I delivered that nudge by claiming I preferred to do business with junior hedge fund managers because I like my men young.

Okay, so I was playing the part of the predatory older woman and doing so because the photo they showed on the firm's website showed no ring on his finger. However, if he thought he was going to score a big investment and then score with a woman trapped in New York for the night he was to be sorely mistaken.

Nevertheless, my lies worked, and I was through the door five minutes later, the faces of Gloria's Gang all pressed against the window of the coffee shop opposite to see me go inside.

Brett was a handsome young man in his late twenties. Sandy brown hair cut short and neat framed a face that reflected the lean body beneath his undoubtedly expensive suit. He shook my hand and tried not to leer – business first though I could tell he was already hoping for pleasure after.

"You'll need to sign in," he explained, guiding me to the reception desk.

The woman there was in her thirties and attractive in a girl-next-door sort of way. The badge on the breast told the world her name: Shanice. She'd taken time with her hair and makeup and smiled at Brett in the hope he might notice.

He didn't.

Mounted to one side of the reception counter, an electronic device controlled people into and out of the building. Brett looked up his firm, and tapped in my name.

"You just need to sign here." Brett stepped back to allow me to make a squiggle on the screen with my right index finger. "And it's right this way."

He wanted to guide me to the elevator, but I'd forced my brain to work overtime so it could come up with a reason to quiz Shanice about the murder and now that I had a thing I could say, I was going to see how she reacted.

Leaving Brett to walk away, I leaned over the counter. "Say, I came by a couple of hours ago and the place was crawling with cops. They said someone reported a murder. Is that true?"

Shanice rolled her eyes. "No. It was three crazy old women from England."

I wanted to see if she would hesitate in giving her answer, and she hadn't. There was something though – when she answered she refused to meet my eyes. Hardly concrete, but I got the impression she was leaving something out.

The elevator pinged quietly.

Waiting by the door, Brett asked, "Are you ready, Mrs Goodman?"

I held up an index finger. "One moment." Staring down at Shanice, I whispered, "Where in the building did it take place? I don't want to find myself in the company of a killer."

This time she relaxed, faint amusement playing across her lips. "No need to worry. It wasn't those guys." She nodded her head toward Brett to be clear who she was talking about.

"Who was it?"

"No one," she replied as though I was now being a bit dense. "The old ladies claimed they saw someone being strangled from the top deck of a sightseeing bus. The only office they could have seen into is Houston Investments and they shut up shop and abandoned their office two days ago. There hasn't been a soul in their office since."

Mentally noting the name, I thanked her for revealing what she could and joined Brett in the elevator.

The hedge fund company resided on the fifth floor. I knew I wanted to explore the second floor and travelling upwards realised I ought to have arranged for Gloria to call me once I was securely in the building. I needed to lose my chaperone, and wasn't going to endure a meeting about investing money when I had so much else to do.

I couldn't very well expose the truth about myself either, so it was time to put the next part of my hastily concocted plan into action.

Inside his office, Brett escorted me into a meeting room where he offered to have refreshments delivered. Seizing my chance, I asked him to pull up opportunities for his top ten high-risk commodities and excused myself to visit the restroom.

Once I was out of sight, I told the lady manning the hedge fund's reception desk I'd forgotten something and needed to return to the building's lobby. She acknowledged my words with a polite murmur, but I was already halfway out the door.

I doubted it would take Brett long to realise I wasn't in the restroom. However, I calculated that I had enough time to take a quick tour of the second floor. My intent was only to demonstrate to Gloria's Gang that I was taking their claims seriously. I would go to the window and wave across the street to show I was in the office where they said the man was strangled before their eyes.

If I found something solid – evidence of a struggle ... well, I would be surprised for one since the police found nothing - but I would contact Captain Danvers and make a report. I could imagine how well that would be received, yet I would do my civic duty and leave it at that. Gloria's Gang could be satisfied one way or the other and I could go about my day.

I found Houston Investments easily enough - coming out of the elevator it was right in front of me. The door was locked as one might expect and it did indeed look completely unoccupied. Faced with a door I could not open, only now did I realise I couldn't go to the window to show the ladies I had gone inside.

Huffing an annoyed sigh, I considered my options. Breaking in was not a sound plan, and I doubted I had the skill to pick the lock even if I possessed the tools to do it, which I didn't.

"Help you, mam?" asked a voice to my left.

Coming though a door marked 'Janitor', a man in his seventies with greying hair and snazzy, blue-framed spectacles, hefted a heavy bunch of keys from which he selected one to lock his door.

"Actually, yes," I reached for my purse. "My boss is thinking about renting this space for the New York branch of his business and I've been waiting ten minutes for Shanice on reception to let me in."

"That girl don't know what day it is half the time," the janitor grumbled.

I took out a pair of twenties. "Could you maybe open the door just so I can see the space and take a couple of pictures. I'll get so much grief if I have to return another time. My boss expects results."

The man took the twenties without a word, the notes vanishing inside a pocket before he lifted the keys.

"I'll need to keep watch," he said. "This lot cleared out so fast they left all their gear behind. Computers and all sorts are just sitting there on the desks."

He wasn't wrong and it struck me as strange that a company going under wouldn't have whoever was chasing the money claiming all the saleable goods to recover some of their losses. That was on my mind until the janitor opened the door.

Then I was thinking about smoke.

The tang of cigar smoke hung invisible yet undeniable in the air inside the office. Shanice told me no one had been in here in weeks and she was either wrong or she was lying. My money was on the latter.

Turning to the man with the keys, I asked, "Did you see anyone in here today?"

"I only just arrived, mam. I come in to start clearing up and work until ten to make sure it's all good to go for the morning. Not that the building is empty when I leave; some of those investment guys stay here until really late. No kind of life if you ask me."

Someone had been in Houston Investment's office today; nothing would convince me otherwise.

Over my shoulder, I announced, "I'm just going to look around and take some pictures." With my phone, I snapped a few pics but what I was really doing was looking for signs of a struggle. I spotted ash on the carpet; big thick flakes in a couple of places, the kind you get from a cigar not a cigarette.

There was no stub from the cigar though, which might conceivably carry the DNA of the alleged killer, and I didn't find anything to suggest a man had fought for and lost his life earlier. If that had happened, the killer must have manoeuvred him into an open space away from the desks, or straightened up afterwards. Either was possible though neither felt likely.

Near the window, having taken my time to get across the room, I made sure to catch the eyes of the three ladies in the coffee shop. Surreptitiously, I waved and got their acknowledgement. Turning around to head back to the exit, I almost bumped into the janitor.

"Sorry," he apologised. "I don't often get to look outside in the daylight. It's quite the city, don't you think?"

"Oh, indeed," I replied to be agreeable, but the pause he gave me worked in my favour: I spotted something else.

On the carpet, there were two marks, long thin tracks where something with small wheels had run more than once. I wasn't sure what to make of it. The short-weave carpet didn't allow for indentations, which meant the wheels had to have run back and forth several times.

Looking around with a frown creasing my face, I spotted another set a few yards away. Standing over them, I had no idea what they represented, but the back of my head itched.

It itched again when I looked up and found a workstation with pictures of someone's children still pinned to the divider between desks.

The staff left here so fast they didn't have time to take their personal belongings?

A cacophony of car horns blared in the street outside, my brain telling me to expect the sound of a crash to follow. No collision came, though I heard a few bellowed insults and expletives – just a day in New York.

Opening the drawer on that desk revealed a few loose change coins, some prescription pills with a name on the bottle, and other items it should have occurred to the owner to take. I read the label: Cindy Lynn.

None of it meant anything, of course. My visit was to prove to myself there had been no murder or, I suppose, explore the possibility that Gloria's Gang were right. The results were inconclusive, but whatever might have happened to shut down the investment firm, there was no sign that a man died in their office today.

The janitor, back at the door, cleared his throat. "I'll need to be getting along now, mam. You about done?"

I nodded, my thoughts elsewhere, and went to the exit. With a thank you to the man whose name I never learned, I called the elevator and hoped to find it empty when it arrived.

Was Brett looking for me? Were they scouring the building? Was I about to be found by security or the cops?

No, it was much worse than that.

Watching

The alert vibrated on his phone and with a frown he checked the screen.

"Now who might you be?" he asked the air for there was one no one around to hear his voice.

Crossing to his workspace, he lowered himself into the wheeled office chair facing his bank of monitor screens with his left leg tucked beneath his body.

Still frowning, he gripped the mouse, guiding the pointer to open the feed for the live video camera he installed in the office of Houston Investments eight days ago. Years of planning and months of work had brought him to his current point, a point that was the penultimate step in achieving unbelievable fortune.

All he had to do now was wait. The deed was done, the patsies were in place ... it felt like he had already gotten away with it.

He hadn't though. Not quite.

Vanishing now would generate questions. Questions would demand answers and if they chose to look, sooner or later they would find him. In order to succeed and not spend the rest of his life looking over his shoulder, it was necessary to wait.

If he waited, the patsies would be found and most likely killed. That didn't concern him one little bit. The lieutenants working beneath the local boss, the big boss's grandson sent to run the local operation, would probably end up dead too. You didn't get to lose this much of the big boss's money and live to tell the tale.

He would be forced to answer some tough questions, but ultimately, he'd made very sure he couldn't be held accountable. All he did was dispense advice and take care of the money – none of the decisions were his.

The office of Houston Investments had been quiet since he took the money until earlier today. When the first crowd arrived this morning, it sent a flutter of panic through his heart until he realised what was going on.

Smirking to himself about his nervous disposition, he watched for a while. They did their thing and left a few hours later. Now there was a new person in the office and something about her face troubled him.

Moving the mouse, he sent the recorded feed to a second screen, replaying the last minutes until her face was looking almost directly at the camera. Snapping a still which he sent to a new folder, he pushed it through a facial recognition program his employers used to identify cops and FBI agents. It was sometimes necessary to target the families of law enforcement officers if they got too close.

The software needed no more than a heartbeat to identify the woman poking around the empty offices of Houston Investments and his blood ran cold.

He ran it again, just to be doubly certain, but he already knew it was right because he'd unconsciously recognised her the first moment he saw her face.

His trembling hand reached for his phone. He knew just who to call. It would cost him, not least because he needed it kept off the books – his employers could never know. However, he could see no choice.

He either dealt with Patricia Fisher as swiftly as possible, or risked her uncovering the truth. Most troubling was the concern that she was there because someone hired her. The renowned sleuth could not be there by accident.

Out of the Frying Pan

The elevator doors swished open to reveal Gloria, Pearl, and Peggy inside. Not that they stayed there. They were already moving forward to escape the steel box's confines before the doors were fully open, barrelling out with their mobility scooters cranked to high revs.

"Oh!" exclaimed Gloria, startled to find me.

She stopped her scooter, but her friends weren't so fast on the uptake so rammed into her as they fought to get out.

"What's going on?" demanded Peggy before looking up and saying, "Oh." Much like Gloria.

"We came to save you," said Pearl. "I see you subdued the miscreant. Good work, Patricia. I'll call the cops."

I'd backed up a step or three to let them out of the elevator, not that Pearl came all the way out. The back wheels of her scooter stayed inside, jamming the doors which bonged insistently each time they tried to close.

I had to go around her sister to grab Pearl's hand before she could start to dial.

"What miscreant? What are you talking about?" I asked.

Gloria answered first. "We saw someone come up behind you, Patricia. A shadow fell across you, and we saw you jump when he attacked from behind."

"That's right," said Pearl. "We figured it was the killer coming back to the scene of the crime to gloat."

"Yeah, or touch himself," said Peggy. When the rest of us all looked at her, she said, "What? That's what serial killers do."

"What are you talking about?" demanded her sister. "How many serial killers do you know to have such an informed opinion?"

The conversation was heading off on a tangent, and the constant bonging noise from the elevator was close to giving me a twitch.

"Can you come out of the elevator, please, Pearl?" I suggested with an insistent, impatient tone.

"Nah, this will stop them from following us," she replied.

"Them?"

The sound of unhappy voices in the stairwell reached my ears.

My eyes flaring, I had to ask, "What did you do?"

What they had done could be viewed as heroic if one chose to be romantic. Alternatively, their actions were criminal and bordering on berserk. Upon seeing what they believed was the killer coming to get me – it had, of course, been the janitor – they left the coffee shop in a hurry, jaywalked ... wait, is it jaywalking if you are on a scooter? Whatever, they jayscootered across the street with drivers forced to swerve to avoid crashing – which explained the cacophony of horns I heard – and swarmed the building.

Shanice apparently shouted and threatened to call the cops for a second time, to which I could fully imagine all three members of Gloria's Gang returning rude gestures.

They invaded the elevator and found me one floor up. Now Shanice had backup and was coming to get them. Waiting to see if it was the police again did not sound like a good plan, so I voted to scarper.

With urgent motions, I got the old ladies back into the elevator, the doors closing a heartbeat before the stairwell door opened and Shanice's voice filled the corridor.

The obvious choice was to head down, but I pressed the button for the next floor and hoped Shanice and whoever was with her would see the direction we were heading. If we went down, they would be able to run confidently down the stairs to cut us off. If we went up and they followed we might get the chance to beat them to the bottom floor when we reversed course.

Obviously, I wouldn't know if the tactic worked until the doors opened on the next floor. When they did, my lungs beginning to ache because nerves were making me hold my breath, but it was clear I had guessed right.

Feet were charging up the stairs, heavy sounding boots echoing in the bare concrete carcass of a stairwell, and loud voices coming closer. I was jabbing the ground floor button from the moment the elevator came to a stop, and the stupid door wouldn't close.

The voices sounded like they were right on top of us, the stairwell doors opening out of the adjacent wall.

"Come on!" I growled, thumbing the 'door close' button for the infinitieth time. The door started to slide shut and at that moment the stairwell doors burst open, a pair of young male cops pausing dramatically in the gap when they caught sight of the faces looking back at them.

"Come and get us, copper!" snarled Gloria, giving the cops a one finger salute just as the gap between the elevator doors closed and we started to move.

We would beat them to the ground floor, but not by much.

Fighting against a need to throttle at least one if not all the ladies presently in my company, I rotated on my heels until I was facing them.

"Come and get us copper?" I repeated Gloria's taunt. "When did we become the bad guys in this scenario?"

Gloria assumed a hurt look. "The bad guys? We're not the bad guys! That's the same two cops who arrested us earlier. They wouldn't listen then, and they won't listen now. We've got to solve this crime together, Patricia."

"Yeah," echoed Pearl. "All for one ..."

"And one for all!" all three cheered together.

Great, now they're the three musketeers. I had to wonder what that made me.

The doors opened with a ping to spill us onto the ground floor. Gloria cranked her throttle wide open, not that I'm suggesting her mobility scooter took off like a scalded cat, but she left the elevator with a determined jolt, her wheels aimed firmly at the building's exit.

I had to grab her handlebars before she escaped me.

"Here, what's going on?" she wanted to know. "I can hear them coming, Patricia. Let's get out of here."

"Yes," I agreed. "But not through the main door and onto the sidewalk where they will be able to catch us ten seconds later."

Thankfully, the ladies could see the alternative door I wanted to use and needed no further encouragement to go through it.

Clattering through the emergency exit set into the wall behind the reception counter, we found ourselves in a grimy back alley running between the buildings. How long would it take the cops to figure out which way we went?

Probably not all that long was my guess.

"Let's keep moving," I suggested. "We need to get out of sight."

If we turned left, we would end up back on the same strip of sidewalk that ran by the front of the office. With right as our only option, that's the way we headed. Directly ahead some hundred yards away, the alley met the next street over, but we found a left turn about twenty yards after setting off. It ran between the high-rise buildings on either side, wheelie bins full of trash acting as obstacles next to fire escape doors and ten yards away a man with his back to us leaned against a wall, smoke drifting upward from a cigarette.

He looked like bad news, and I wanted to reverse direction already. However, no sooner did we turn the corner than the sound of a door clattering open echoed down the alley behind us. Voices followed, the cops if I wasn't mistaken – we were right to get out of sight, but were far from safe yet.

The man with the cigarette dropped it and ground it beneath his shoe before elbowing his way back through a door to get inside.

"I'm going to check this way," came from behind us, one of the cops deciding to scope out the alley – they were chasing a pack of old ladies and probably figured they couldn't get far.

As quietly as I could, I urged Gloria's Gang toward the smoker's door. He hadn't pulled it shut behind him and it rested temptingly against the frame, open just a crack.

Slipping inside, I went last so I could pull the door to and watched though the thin slit to make sure the cop checked and then moved on. When I felt the coast was clear we would leave again, and this time vacate the area.

Returning to the ship and staying there for the rest of the New York visit was starting to sound like a good idea. However, as is typical for me, when I turned around to beckon the ladies, they were nowhere to be seen.

"Gloria!" I hissed, my tone urgent, impatient, and annoyed. "Gloria!"

No answer. I tried calling the others too, but unwilling to raise my voice, I couldn't make them hear me.

Muttering obscenities under my breath, I set off to find them. I was in the back of a building, lost in the corridors linking different storerooms and such. There were mattresses of every shape and size stacked in the corridors and inside the rooms I passed. I could hear voices – male voices, not that I could make out what they were saying - and thought it odd that I was able to walk around without bumping into anyone.

Rounding a corner, the volume of the voices rose, and I found Gloria, Pearl, and Peggy with their scooters all in a line. They were peering around a corner to spy on someone.

"What are you doing?" I demanded to know, my angry voice nothing more than a whisper.

Peggy lifted a finger to her lips. "Shhh. We're listening."

"They're talking about drugs," revealed Pearl. "It's some kind of gang meeting."

Gloria turned her head slightly to look at me. "They're negotiating territory and prices. That fellow," she aimed a finger, "I think he's the boss. He sounds like he's in charge, but there's some issue with cashflow. He's demanding the other bunch hand over the product and wait for payment."

My heart jackhammered in my chest, and I felt positively sick. Tugging at Gloria's coat, I whispered, "You lot are completely nuts! We need to get out of here before someone sees us!"

"Too late for that, Miss," said a voice from behind me.

Completely Senile

I turned around so fast I almost left my eyeballs behind.

Filling the corridor was the man I saw smoking in the alley. I could tell you about his height and features and stuff, but my attention was too firmly fixed on the boxy machine gun he held to take anything much else in.

"Oh, here's one of them now," said Peggy. "You're busted, mister! The cops are already on their way."

"No they're not!" I blurted. "No, they're not! Don't listen to her. She's completely senile. We wandered in here by mistake. Haven't heard anything. Haven't seen anything. We'll just be going now. Don't worry, we can see ourselves out."

"Completely senile?" repeated Peggy, unhappy at the suggestion.

Believing she was going to start a discussion on the subject of her mental faculties, I was glad when the smoker cut over the top of her.

"Move." He jabbed the muzzle of his gun at us. "Wrong place, wrong time, girls. Nothing personal."

Furiously my mind scrambled, but with the gun in my face and my bladder threatening to rebel, I backed up a pace. Gloria's Gang, the three old ladies sitting astride their mobility scooters were yet to move so I bumped into the nearest of them.

The gunman's expression switched gear from unpleasant sneer to evil snarl.

"Move. I won't ask again."

Right behind me, Pearl said, "Can you move to your left a little, Patricia. You're blocking my aim."

I complied without my brain connecting the dots to realise what her words meant and the moment my feet moved, two darts shot past the side of my face on an upward trajectory.

The darts embedded in the gunman's forehead, dispensing however many thousands of volts a taser gun can deliver. He spasmed, my eyes going wide as I recognised what was about to happen.

Gloria's Gang were fine; they were all sitting down. I, however, was about to get shot.

With a squeal of fright, I dropped to the floor a millisecond before the man's jerky finger pulled the trigger. The air above my head exploded with noise, bullets ripping through the air as he fell backward.

Someone yelled, "It's a double cross!" and yet more shots were fired, this time coming from the group of men Gloria and the twins had chosen to spy on.

"It's the cops!" and "Get outta here!" rang out among the confused shouts as the drug gangs, or whatever they were, ran to get away.

The last juice from Pearl's taser discharged into the gunman and he hit the floor unconscious. Landing with a thump like a thick wooden board being dropped, his gun clattered across the floor and he farted.

If ever there was a time to be somewhere else, this was it, but getting back to the fire door we came in through was blocked by the gunman's body. I could step over it, but would need to drag it to one side if the girls on their scooters were going to escape the same way.

The fog of digested garlic sausage stench rising from the prone body at my feet wasn't quite enough to put me off manhandling him, but the sound of the cops heading our way was. They'd heard the shots and were reacting. Of course they were.

Spinning around and back on my feet, I urged, "Quick! Go that way! Find a way out!"

I needn't have worried for Gloria's Gang were already moving, their scooters whipping around the corner and out into the open loading bay space beyond.

Horror gripped me the moment I caught sight of what I expected to be an empty space devoid of the men it housed a few moments earlier. Two of them had gotten caught in the crossfire and were leaking vital fluids onto the cold concrete.

One was trying to sit up and despite the danger he presented, I went to him. His weapon, a small automatic handgun, was a few feet away and out of his reach.

Gloria wheeled right up to his feet. "Not looking so cocky now, are you?" she cackled.

"Gloria, he's hurt!" I growled, doing what I could to stem the blood coming from his chest. "Make yourself useful and check on the other man."

"This one's a goner," said Peggy, bumping into his head with her scooter to demonstrate the lack of life.

The sound of feet heading our way became voices a moment later.

"Hands! I want to see hands from everyone!" yelled one of the cops.

I twisted around so they could see my face, but I didn't raise my hands.

"He's been shot in the chest!" I shouted while praying Gloria, Peggy, and Pearl wouldn't do anything stupid like trying to resist, or produce another taser to employ. Where the heck had they found that thing anyway?

Chief of Police

More police arrived as one might imagine they would. Paramedics too who pronounced both victims deceased at the scene. Taken to one side by a pair of detectives, we were grilled on who we were and how we came to be inside the storeroom.

It took almost no time at all for the cops to identify me. All I had to do was say my name.

"Patricia Fisher?" Detective Rogers repeated my name. "The broad on the cruise ship? That thing with the Godmother and the Alliance of Families?"

"One and the same," I admitted, unsure whether I ought to feel proud or be embarrassed.

It turned out the loading bay was for a place selling beds and mattresses. The owner was long thought to be a connected hoodlum who avoided the great purge that followed me exposing the Godmother and the total collapse of her criminal empire. The owner was nowhere to be found and had probably chosen to make for the hills when the first shots were fired.

The man I attempted to save had nothing on him to identify who he was, but the second dead man was part of a gang operating out of Queens. Calling themselves the New Initiative, they had moved to occupy a dominant spot in the New York underworld. Again, this turf warring could be traced back to me removing the Godmother. With her alliance in place there had been little rivalry between the families. The vacuum that followed her fall sucked in new players too numerous to count.

It was probably why Captain Danvers looked so stressed.

I felt bad.

Time ticked away, a crime scene unit arriving to process the scene as we were led to an incident control area outside.

The man Pearl tasered was up and on his feet; we got to see him being led away in cuffs. Unsurprisingly, the detectives wanted to know how it was that he came to be tasered in the first place and that led to a confession.

Pearl handed over her taser. Peggy had one too, the pair of them having bought them only a few hours earlier from a pawn shop they passed. Apparently that's not even legal and the cops were more interested in the name of the shop and its location than they were in the ladies possessing the weapons.

"Anything else, ladies?" Detective Rogers asked, a raised eyebrow enough to show he thought he'd seen everything, but taser toting grannies was new.

Peggy shook her head. "Nope."

"Not a thing," agreed Pearl.

"I didn't get one," said Gloria, sounding thoroughly disappointed.

"Are we free to go?" I asked, familiar enough with the process to believe we would be sent on our way now they had our statements.

Rogers shared a look with his partner, Richards, both men amused by my question.

"There's just the small matter of breaking and entering to deal with, ladies," said Rogers.

Ah, yes. The cops who chased us around the Roosevelt Building were the first on scene here too. They dealt with the more pressing matter of bodies shot full of holes first, but that did nothing to eliminate the earlier issue.

"Captain Danvers is on his way here," Richards let us know.

Just what I needed. Would he throw the book at me? I promised I wouldn't stick my nose in and at the time I'd truly meant it. Would he go through with his promise to arrest me? Surely not.

Maybe though. I weighed up my odds and didn't like them.

Annoyed at how my day had turned out, I leaned against some mattresses piled in one corner of the loading bay and looked out through the open roller door. The sun had already given up for the day and it was hours ago when I promised Barbie I would be with her soon.

Shocked to not have missed calls or messages from her, I chose to dial her number myself.

"Patty? Did you and Alistair lose track of time?" she teased good-naturedly.

"Not exactly," I huffed out a sigh. "Alistair had to return to the ship. We were only ashore together for a couple of hours. Not even long enough to get a hotdog," I lamented, my belly choosing that moment to remind me I hadn't eaten since breakfast.

'The museum shuts in an hour, Patty. Are you likely to get here before then?"

"You're still there?" I asked, my voice incredulous. "Barbie that's your whole day. You didn't need to spend it all doing research."

"Oh, it's been fun, Patty, don't worry. Hideki knows we will be back here in a few months and he's almost as much of a geek as me. Plus, it's really fascinating stuff. One of the assistant curators came by a few hours ago to check on us and he pretty much scoffed at the idea the San José could be anywhere but the bottom of the ocean. If only he knew, eh?"

"Well, yes. Okay, if you're sure it's not ruining your shore leave ..."

Barbie said, "We've learned so much today. I think we need a session in your cabin tonight – we can all put our heads together and see if we can't manage to piece some of this mystery together. I'd rather get to the bottom of what happened to Finn Murphy than risk running into the fake Professor Noriega again."

So would I. He came at us with murderous intent and was almost certainly behind the theft of the treasure from my safe, albeit he sent another man to get it. Identifying him so he could be brought to justice was one of the biggest drivers dictating we commit time to finding how and why Finn Murphy was killed.

"Where are they?" Captain Danvers voice cut through the hubbub of conversation, making me wince.

Turning my head slightly to see the irate senior police officer approaching, I said to Barbie, "I've got to go. Are you leaving now?"

"No. They will have to kick us out when they want to shut the place. We'll go for dinner then though, so Hideki gets to see something of New York."

I promised to get to the museum to meet with them if humanly possible and put my phone away just as Captain Danvers arrived.

He looked about ready to have a heart attack.

"Mrs Fisher." He stopped a yard from me, fists balled on his hips as he looked along the line of ladies waiting to be lectured at volume. "Mrs Fisher, can you give me one good reason why I don't lock the four of you in a cell until your ship is due to sail?"

I was about to answer, when he carried on talking.

"Not only did you immediately return to the same building your ..." he fought to find a word that suited, "accomplices invaded earlier today, you then broke in again using subterfuge, insulted two of my officers, and resisted arrest by evading them when they ordered you to stop."

Peggy cackled and nudged her sister. "Yeah! It was brilliant!"

I shot her a look that ought to have set her hair alight. Mercifully, she took the hint and folded one lip over the other.

"Captain Danvers there is something very screwy going on in the Roosevelt Building. Houston Investments closed unexpectedly two days ago according to the lady working the building's reception desk. When they cleared out, they went so fast the people working there didn't even stop to gather personal possessions. My ... friends," I almost called them accomplices myself, "witnessed a murder in the exact same office earlier today."

"No, they did not!" Captain Danvers argued instantly.

"Yes, we did!" snapped Gloria, quickly echoed by Peggy and Pearl.

I offered kindly eyes to the harassed police captain. "I believe they saw something. I know your officers didn't find a body or any sign of a struggle and neither did I, but something *is* going on there."

"And?" Danvers demanded.

And? The question reverberated around my head. And what? What was I asking him to do? Divert resources to investigate a supposed murder no one else knew anything about. There's a simple rule about murder: no body equals no murder.

Since there was no dead body, there was nothing to investigate. At least not for the police.

Feeling heat in my cheeks, I looked Captain Danvers directly in the eyes.

"I apologise for the mess. You're right, this is none of my business and I should have left it to the professionals to investigate." I'm no more a fan of humble pie than anyone else on the planet, but I was in the wrong. Or, at least, I couldn't yet prove I was right and that amounted to the same thing.

Danvers nodded his head just a little, acknowledging my words and giving them some consideration. A few seconds ticked by before he spoke again.

Waving an arm in a sweeping motion to take in the scene behind him, he said, "As you can see, I have my hands full. I want you to believe that is the only reason I am letting you go."

He was letting us go. Thank goodness.

"Be warned though," he jerked a finger at me and then each of the ladies in turn, "one more false move and I'll have no choice but to incarcerate the lot of you and I won't even feel bad about it. In fact, I think I'll sleep a lot better knowing you cannot cause any more drama." He glared at me, looking like he expected me to say something in response. "Well?" he demanded. "What are you waiting for? Get out of here!"

Seriously concerned one of my elderly female companions might voice her thoughts, I flared my eyes at them and hitched my head in the direction of the exit.

As one, the ladies turned the keys on their scooters and pulled forward, turning right to drive away in a single file.

I paused to say, "Thank you. Please get some rest, Captain Danvers, you look exhausted."

A tired laugh escaped his lips. "That's because I have Agatha Christie's leftovers running riot in my city. God save me from amateur sleuths."

I had a selection of parting comments to fire back, but held my tongue. Had he been more generous – I *am* a professional sleuth – I might have let things lie. Instead, his words started a fire inside me that was only going to be quenched when I handed over whoever was behind the mysterious murder Gloria's Gang witnessed.

Dinner with Friends

G loria and the twins were just as hungry as me and ready to ditch their quest for
justice in favour of sustenance.

"Where should we go, ladies?" asked Gloria. "Where is good to eat in New York?"

"Beats me," said Peggy. "It's my first time here."

"Mine too," admitted Pearl. "But I'm willing to bet just about anywhere will have good food. Let's see what the phone says?" Whipping out her phone, the octogenarian proceeded to baffle me with her mastery of its applications. In seconds she had a list of all the restaurants in the area and was pulling up menus with Gloria and Peggy craning their necks to see the tiny screen.

"You'll be all right without me?" I asked. "What's your plan for after dinner?"

Gloria rapped the controls of her scooter with a bony knuckle.

"Battery won't last much longer."

"Nor mine," agreed Peggy.

Gloria looked up at me. "I guess we'll be heading back to the ship once we've eaten. The sights and sounds of late night New York might have enthralled me years ago, but it's of

51

no interest now. I'm looking forward to a cup of hot cocoa and a few more chapters of the book I'm reading. What about you?"

I checked my watch. "I'm going to try to catch up with Barbie." I looked about to see if there was a cab. Six passed me by in the next two seconds. "I'll see you all back at the ship then?" I wanted to confirm they wouldn't try any more foolish shenanigans tonight, but to do so would plant the idea in their heads. Instead, I was going to hope they managed to get back without being arrested.

Splitting to set off in different directions, I needed only to raise my arm to get a yellow cab to pull up to the kerb. Moments later I was on my way to the museum.

Relaxing in the spacious, if a little soft and spongey, confines of the cab's backseat, I allowed my thoughts to drift back to Houston Investments. A hedge fund firm that suddenly closed might not be unusual – I genuinely didn't know, but my understanding of such dealings was that they existed to provide a high return for their investors and to do so meant taking risks.

Getting it wrong and going bust, if that was what had happened, sounded innocent enough, but to leave so fast no one had a chance to clear out their desks triggered a warning buzzer in my head. Combine that with Shanice lying about people going in there today and Gloria's Gang reporting a murder in progress made the investment firm the focus of my investigation.

I chose to stick with the assumption that Gloria's Gang were right about what they saw. Otherwise, despite the weird absence of the firm's staff, there was nothing to investigate.

Was the murdered man someone who worked at Houston Investments? How would I figure that out? Recalling something Barbie showed me about company website structures, I tapped 'Houston Investments' into a search engine on my phone.

I got a bunch of hits, the name alone returning four different firms which I was able to narrow down as only one displayed a New York address. It was hard to see on the tiny screen, not least because the streets of New York are pockmarked with so many holes a blind man could drive around using the divots as a form of Braille and my phone bounced about as much as the rest of me. However, I found the list of employees, each with a photograph. Wishing I could have thought of this when Gloria's Gang were still around to look at it, I made a mental note to catch up with them later.

If they recognised the man they saw being strangled, maybe it would give me a starting point.

I was looking through the firm's details: history, marketing blurb, and such when the cabbie pulled to the left and stopped.

Looking up, I was surprised to discover we were already at the museum. I handed over some notes and was barely on the pavement when the taxi roared away again.

There were lights on, but a quick glance at my watch showed me I had only a couple of minutes left to get inside – not enough to find my friends. Ten seconds later, when I was looking around to spot a bar where I could await their exit, I saw Barbie's shock of blonde hair coming down the stone steps from the grand entrance. Hideki, Martin Baker, and Deepa Bhukari were with her, the two couples each holding their partner's hands.

The sight shot a small pang of annoyance through me. I was supposed to be enjoying a short romantic break with Alistair; one we had been planning for more than a week. Instead I was alone, got barely two hours with him when we did get off the ship, and I hadn't heard from him since he'd been forced to go back.

Telling myself to stop whining, I waved and called to the foursome eagerly striding down the stairs to the street below.

"Patty!" yelled Barbie, exuberant as always.

They already had a table booked in an Italian place a block over. We walked to get there, the chilly New York air making me wish I had an extra layer, but the service, atmosphere, and the food was worth it.

"So, they saw someone get strangled?" Hideki asked.

I'd started out asking them about what their day of research uncovered, but the conversation got turned about somehow because we were all now discussing Houston Investments and Gloria's Gang.

I shrugged in reply. "I'm willing to believe they saw something. I don't know if it was a murder or not though."

Barbie and Deepa, sitting opposite me and together like conspirators, were on their phones.

"There's nothing in the papers about Houston Investments shutting down," said Deepa. "Oh, wait, here's a little something." She began to read, "William Chalice remains unavailable for comment amid demands from investors to explain why they have stopped trading. Rumours are rife that the fledgling firm might have suffered at the hands of a cybercriminal. That's in the Wall Street Journal," she explained the source, speaking to the group though her attention stayed on her phone. "The article goes on to say the Journal's own investigators spoke to multiple investors with their money in Houston Investments and they all reported concern, but that their money appeared to be where it should be. It makes it sound like their issue is that they cannot access it because the firm have stopped answering the phones."

"Someone who hacked into their computers?" I questioned. "I thought financial institutions were protected against all that sort of thing these days. Don't they have to be?"

Barbie looked up from her phone. "Architects create new systems everyday to keep one step ahead of the criminals who want to make easy money, but deconstructing a system will always be possible. There will always be a way to get through the firewalls. You're not wrong though, this is unusual. Whoever was responsible for protecting their investors ought to get fired."

Thinking of something else, I remarked, "If they got hacked, the thief would take all the money, right?

With a frown on his face, Hideki asked, "The rumours will have come from somewhere." He frowned, a look of deep concentration suggesting he was trying to work something out. "If the Journal thinks Houston Investments got hacked, how come their investors say their money is still there?"

No one had an answer.

Dinner arrived, plates of pasta and pizza in plentiful portions. The air stank of wonderous garlic, butter, herbs, and rich ragu. I drank wine because it paired better with my meal than a gin and tonic would, and the conversation lapsed while we ate.

When people were finished and the waiter returned to collect the plates, I asked about the San José again.

Martin Baker led the response. "We're no closer to knowing where the San José went, but coming from a position of being utterly certain it wasn't sunk by the British in 1708 allows us to approach it in a way I doubt many others have."

His wife, Deepa, took over. "Finn Murphy is likely to be the key to unravelling the final location of the ship. Artefacts and letters have cropped up over the years, reports from persons who claim to have been part of the crew, but that's all too far in the past to be of much help. I think we should look more closely at Finn Murphy and find out where he was in the weeks prior to his death."

"I agree," Martin cut in, angling a sly smile at his wife who was just as eager to tell the tale. "Lieutenant Bernadino Alvarez might have been the real thing, or could have been a criminal assuming a fake identity. There is just no way to know."

"Regardless," Barbie took up the report, "none of the artefacts give us a start point to look for the ship and the treasure Finn Murphy obviously found. I ..." she paused to check with her companions, "we believe retracing Finn Murphy's steps is the most likely route to success."

I drew in a slow breath through my nose, considering her statement. Finn Murphy found the treasure. Whether it was still with the ship or somewhere else, he found it. If I could figure out where he boarded the ship, we might be halfway home.

"Okay, so we know roughly when he died from the autopsy report." Hideki gave a slight nod of his head as he was the one who examined the body. "That gives us a location to work back from." I thought about that for a second. "That's not helpful though because we have no way of knowing where and when he boarded the ship."

"There will be clues, Patty," Barbie reassured me. "You always figure it out."

"What about the bug in his hair?" asked Deepa, referring to a small beetle Hideki found during the autopsy. It was dead, the carcass trapped in Finn Murphy's matted hair and was so super rare it could be found on one island only.

"Lucanus punctatum," said Hideki.

Barbie shot him some side eye. "Now is not the time for Harry Potter spells, darling."

Hideki rolled his eyes.

"That's the Latin name for the bug, babe. It is indigenous to the island of Asreb which is part of the Spanish city of Melilla on the North African coast."

Barbie grinned devilishly. "I love it when you use big words." Turning serious, she added, "The ship doesn't stop there though. Does it?"

Martin shook his head. "Not to my knowledge. I don't think the port is deep enough for even a small cruise ship. And that's Melilla I'm talking about, not Asreb."

"But he was there," I concluded. "It could be the location of the San José for all we know."

"It's uninhabited," Hideki added. "The perfect place for a ship to go unnoticed for three hundred years."

Martin argued, "Someone would have seen it at some point."

His opinion was valid, but it was one I could counter. "Not if it sank." That got everyone's attention. "Let's assume the crew mutinied and took the ship full of treasure. They want to return to Spain, but cannot arrive with the ship and the treasure if they want to keep it for themselves. They have to go somewhere else to break it down and divide it up, but having sailed across the Atlantic, they get caught in a storm and the ship sinks in shallow water just off the coast of Asreb. Maybe Melilla was their intended port and they failed just a few nautical miles from safety."

Around the table, my friends were nodding their heads thoughtfully.

Barbie said, "Finn Murphy might have found it by accident. Maybe he was there scuba diving by himself ..."

"Or with a partner he murdered to avoid sharing," countered Deepa.

I had yet another theory. "Or he ran out on the friend who then tracked him to the ship and killed him."

As theories go it had no basis whatsoever, yet it pieced together the things we knew and made sense of them.

"Yeah, but," started Martin, "that still fails to explain how he got on the ship. The ship doesn't stop at Melilla."

Silence fell over the table once more. It was a mystery and no mistake, but not one we were going to solve tonight.

We ate dessert; a large slice of tiramisu for me, and to my surprise the vote was to head back to the Aurelia. Apparently, research is tiring, and everyone wanted to get an early night. Hideki was back on duty tomorrow, the rotation between doctors on call a continual thing. Martin and Deepa were free but there was always something to deal with on board such a giant vessel.

For my part, I wanted to get a bath and rescue my dogs from Molly and Anders, two more of my team who volunteered to have my pair of miniature dachshunds because taking them ashore into a city like New York can be awfully restrictive – they are not welcome inside a museum for a start. Once that was done, I hoped to salvage some of my planned day with Alistair. I'd eaten, but maybe we could snuggle up and watch a movie.

Hugo Lockhart

H ugo Lockhart found it was all he could do not to rub his hands with glee. Captured inside his head was an image of his bank balance. There had never been so much money in his account and there probably never would be again.

It wasn't a fortune. It's not like he could retire and live out his days in paradise, but he could put down a deposit on an apartment of his own and move out of his mother's place finally. That his wife left him and took all his money remained a subject he could not dwell on without becoming irrationally angry even now, five years after it happened.

Sensing his anger rising, he forced himself to breathe and relax. Closing his eyes, Hugo tilted his head to one side then the other, trying to loosen the tension in his shoulders.

Until a few hours ago, Senor Silvestre was nothing more than a shadowy figure he'd heard from once. The man put money in his bank every month and he'd never had to do anything for it. Until a few hours ago.

A few hours ago he was reminded just how much money he'd taken from a man he'd never met. Senor Silvestre gave simple, easy to follow instructions, and delivered them with a tone that expected compliance. Expected compliance with an undertone of unpleasantness if Hugo chose to deviate from the simple, easy to follow instructions.

That was why he was sitting in the lobby of the Waldorf Astoria hotel feeling very much out of place. He bet every single person staying here gave away more in tips over a weekend than he earned in a year.

In many ways he was thankful it was after three in the morning. It meant there was no one about. The dapperly-dressed gentleman at the concierge desk had asked if he needed anything more than once. To Hugo's ears the subtle subtext of his question sounded more like, 'Why are you here making this fine establishment look scruffy?'.

His discomfort aside, Hugo kept nodding off and would wake to find he was dribbling onto the ornate chair in which he sat. He would be tired when he got to work, and his back was getting stiff, but Senor Silvestre was very clear that Hugo would wait in the lobby for his arrival.

So that was what he was doing.

Hugo woke yet again when the doorman's footsteps scurried to respond to a car pulling up out front. By the time the doors opened inward, Hugo was sitting up and a sleeve had been employed to tidy the drool from his chin.

A small man walked in. Hugo judged his height to be five feet and eight inches and unlike some short men he did not appear to be wearing any kind of heel to add back some of the height nature chose to deny him.

A moment later, a giant followed in his wake. Hugo's eyes flared at the sight. Not just tall, the man was broad too, his shoulders and chest displaying the muscle beneath even in the suit the man wore. Was he seven feet tall? Hugo doubted he would get much change if he wasn't, and the man's head was shaved down to shiny skin that made it look like a giant bowling ball.

In his hands a basketball would simply vanish.

Hugo gulped, certain the shorter of the pair was Senor Silvestre. Nerves gripped him, a sudden desire to be elsewhere spurring his legs to twitch, but he couldn't quite get his feet to move.

The shorter man was at the reception desk, being dealt with by the ever-efficient staff there. Behind him, casting a giant shadow, the huge man turned his head to look Hugo's way.

In the recesses of his mind, a terrified voice sniggered that Hugo should be relieved the turning head didn't sound like two pieces of stone pillar being rubbed against each other – the man was just a man even if he did look like a terminator.

Receiving his room keys with a nod and a smile, the shorter man also looked his way. However, unlike his giant companion (Hugo's mind labelled him as a henchman) Senor Silvestre came to greet him.

"Mr Lockhart. Thank you for agreeing to meet with me at such short notice." He gripped Hugo's unresisting hand and pumped it eagerly. "I hope you have not been waiting long."

"No, no, not long," Hugo lied, trying hard to look at the man in front of his face and not at the giant who he would swear was yet to blink.

"Very good, but you look tired, Mr Lockhart, please accompany me up to my suite. We have matters to discuss."

Those were the exact same words the Spaniard used earlier on the phone. 'Matters to discuss'. What did that mean? He had been paid in advance, the years of monthly payments now hanging like a noose around Hugo's neck, and he was to be rewarded again now for assisting Senor Silvestre with ... something.

The giant with the luggage, which he refused to give up to the bellboy, crossed to the elevator where he waited for his master. Senor Silvestre was on his way there too, that Hugo might refuse to follow him to his suite a concept that probably never crossed his mind.

He was proven right too, Hugo traipsing nervously after the Spaniard like a puppy on a leash.

However, when Hugo left the hotel some twenty-seven minutes later, it was with a skip in his step. Yet again the image of his bank balance came to mind. An extra ten thousand dollars! All he had to do was help Senor Silvestre to find out what the blonde woman and her party knew.

That was going to be easy.

He already had a plan to get them back to the museum; it would only take a phone call to explain that he'd found some additional artefacts. That was technically a lie, but the blonde ... what was her name? Hugo had to rack his brain to recall it, 'Barbie' popping into his head from somewhere a few seconds later. Barbie would never know Hugo was lying because Senor Silvestre provided him with artefacts to show her.

The museum curator part of his personality was thoroughly curious about the items he now held in his possession. Gold coins, a sextant, and the diary of the captain. How Senor Silvestre came by the items he would not say. Nor would he comment on why he so fervently wanted to know what the blonde knew.

Feeling like he was caught up on the fringe of a fantastic adventure from a spy novel, there was one other matter tickling Hugo's brain. Senor Silvestre showed him a photograph of a blonde woman and asked him to confirm she was the one who came to the museum.

However, the photograph was not of Barbie and that seemed to throw the Spaniard.

Barbie was in her early twenties if Hugo was any judge. Certainly her chest was yet to begin its steady descent south; he'd noticed her impressive rack and cringed a little as he remembered fighting not to stare at it. The photograph Senor Silvestre showed him, however, was of a much older woman.

There was something familiar about her face, like he'd seen it on TV or something, but whoever she was, she had to be thirty years older than Barbie. Thankfully, Hugo's description of the busty blonde seemed to quell Senor Silvestre's concerns; it wasn't what he'd expected to hear but was acceptable.

Not that Hugo cared. He was being handsomely rewarded for doing nothing illegal. Hailing a cab, he mused that he could afford the fare for once.

Breakfast News

A listair made himself free the previous evening and I was most pleased to awaken to the sound of his gentle breathing as he slept on the pillow next to mine.

The ship was sick, that was his reason for returning to the Aurelia yesterday afternoon. Commander Philips, the chief engineer, could fix it, but I learned from Alistair that the ship would not be able to sail tonight as was planned.

Telling the passengers they were stuck in New York for an extended period was a job for the captain and no one else, hence his return to the ship to see if anything could be done to avoid the issue.

It could not.

I didn't fully understand the problem, but it was linked to the sabotage a former deputy captain, Commander Schooner, inflicted a few months ago. Something undetected or undetectable had remained dormant until now. It was critical and needed to be fixed before the Aurelia went back to sea.

The upshot was that Alistair still couldn't accompany me into New York. Purple Star Cruise Line ships run on schedule so the fact that we would not was a big thing. It gave me time to focus my energy on the San José mystery and to delve into the Houston Investments case.

If you asked me to articulate quite why I wanted to solve the second one, I would have a hard time explaining. Even to myself. In fact, lying there in Alistair's embrace, some of the fire I felt the previous evening, after Captain Danvers made such cutting remarks, faded away.

Did I really need to pursue it? Obviously not. Had the alleged crime happened on board the Aurelia, I would have been all over it and pushing my team to find the answers. That wasn't the case though, and I felt a subtle tension leave my body when I chose to let it go.

I hadn't even been aware it was making me tense.

Alistair stayed with me for breakfast, my butler Jermaine making omelette Arnold Bennett for each of us.

My dachshunds, Anna and Georgie, a mother and daughter, fussed around my stool set at the breakfast bar - they wanted a plate to lick and who could blame them? It was delicious.

I was just tucking into the last bite when someone started to hammer at my door.

Anna and Georgie burst into action. They barked and ran, their tiny bodies whipping across the carpet at a speed which, quite frankly, defies logic.

Jermaine dried his hands and walked sedately and calmly across my suite to get to the door. To be clear, we didn't need him to answer the door to see who was outside, Gloria's voice penetrated through the solid wood and walls like a foghorn on a misty night.

Her voice was joined by Peggy and Pearl's, the twins adding their volume to the demand to be let in.

Anna and Georgie had to back up when Jermaine opened the door; the ladies mobility scooters were charged up and moving fast. Running to get away from them, my dogs returned to their quest for food.

I gave them my plate to lick and slid off the barstool to greet my guests.

Halfway across my suite's central living space, Gloria began to rant, "He's in the papers! I told you we saw him get murdered!" She had a newspaper in her hands, but was too agitated in her movements for me to be able to see it in any detail.

"Yeah! The cops will have to take us seriously now," added Peggy.

I raised my hands, begging the ladies to be calm and slow down.

"Who's dead? What are you trying to tell me?" I begged to know.

"The man we saw being strangled yesterday. His body was found last night. It's in the paper!" Gloria finally put the paper down, spreading it on the coffee table so I could see.

Alistair and Jermaine joined me which made six of us all staring at a small article on page three of the New York Times.

Pearl had her phone out and was trying to push it into my palm.

"The online article provides more detail."

Once again unable to avoid the case, I began to read.

The dead man's name was Chet Kowalski, that vital snippet of detail appearing on the second line. "It says he was shot," I pointed out, my eyes twitching left to right as they danced over the words. "Shot not strangled."

"He must have fought his attacker off," said Peggy. "We saw him being strangled, but the bus moved forward, and we lost sight of him and the killer. He must have escaped only to be tracked down and shot a few hours later."

"We were right," Gloria reminded the room. "That's the important thing. I cannot wait to see that Captain Danvers again. Ooh, he's got a stern talking to coming his way."

I doubted that was a good move to make, but I couldn't argue with their logic regarding Mr Kowalski's demise.

"You're sure this is the same man you saw?" I challenged.

Gloria smirked. "He was right by the window when the bus stopped in traffic. Couldn't have been more than ten feet between us. I'll never forget his face."

I glanced at Alistair who teased, "I guess I don't need to worry about you having nothing to do today." His day would get sucked up dealing with passengers and their concerns regarding the ship's late departure. He believed I was going to put on my sleuthing shoes and set out to solve the mystery. Half an hour ago, I'd been lying in bed content to leave the case alone. Now I wasn't so sure I could because Gloria's Gang were going to be hard to dissuade from getting involved.

"Coffee, madam?" asked Jermaine.

I nodded absentmindedly, my thoughts on the dead man and who might have killed him. Did he work at Houston Investments? Was his murder something to do with why the firm shut down so suddenly last week?

Snapping out of the little cloud of thoughts filling my brain, I spun around to face my butler.

"Sweetie, do you have plans for the day?"

"Yes, madam, I intend do to whatever you desire."

It was a typical Jermaine answer. He enjoys being my butler, but he is so much more than that and I count him as one of my dearest and closest friends. He is kind and sweet. He can cook and bake like a professional chef. He is loyal, disciplined, and efficient, and if needed he can beat a roomful of men to a pulp without so much as breaking a sweat.

Thanking him with my eyes, I said, "I believe I will have need of you today, sweetie. Dress for a day in the city." I said the words knowing he would reappear in a pinstripe suit and tie with oxford shoes topped off with a black umbrella and bowler hat. His favourite fictional character is *Steed* from the *Avengers*, but he wore it well and looked smart rather than ridiculous.

Not that I was about to put on an Emma Peel catsuit to make up the other half of the fictional crime-fighting duo. I'm happy enough with my figure, but I'm no Diana Rigg.

Gloria tugged at the sleeve of my dressing gown. "You're going to help us catch the killer then? To heck with the cops, we'll solve the case ourselves?"

The look of hope in her eyes would have been enough to tip the balance if I hadn't already decided. Part of me wanted to show off; presenting Captain Danvers and the chief of police with a case they could close just to demonstrate I was no amateur – I was still glowering about Captain Danvers' last remark. However, I also felt sorry for the man, so if I could in some small way alleviate a little of his stress by reducing his workload, I would do so.

Facing the three old ladies, I said, "Yes, I am. I need to shower and get dressed first, and then we will need to examine what we know and dig into Houston Investments."

"Shall I assemble your team, madam?" asked Jermaine, returning from the open plan kitchen to hand me a mug of coffee.

I accepted it with a nod of thanks. "Yes, please, but only if they are free. They all have shore leave with the exception of Hideki and I've no wish to disturb whatever plans they might have made."

When I came out of my bedroom twenty minutes later, the drained coffee mug in one hand and my dachshunds trailing behind me, I found Barbie chatting with Jermaine. Also present was Ensign Molly Lawrence, a twenty-one-year-old girl from England who used to be my housemaid until I brought her on the cruise ship and opened her eyes to what her life could be like. Sitting next to her on my couch was Lieutenant Anders Pippin. From South Africa, the slight man was dating Molly and had been part of my team from before I officially had one.

Sitting opposite them, thirty-one-year-old Ensign Sam Chalk waved at me. He's a bit goofy, but he's also brilliant and brave and possesses so many wonderful qualities that the team would be weakened without him.

"Morning, Mrs Fisher," he grinned at me.

Finally, standing behind Sam's wingback chair like the oversized sentinel he is, Lieutenant Schneider dipped his head to greet me. He's a six-foot goodness knows what Austrian with muscle to spare and has assumed a kind of big brother role with Sam.

I said, "Good morning, everyone," as I joined them.

Martin and Deepa were absent, and I was glad. They didn't need to be involved as well and I hoped they were going to enjoy a day sightseeing together.

Barbie looked up and came toward me, an open laptop in her hands.

"Chet Kowalski didn't work at Houston Investments," she said, placing the laptop on a desk just behind the arrangement of couches and chairs. "He was a waiter."

I'd not read enough of the news column to see if that information was listed, but had no reason to doubt my blonde friend's claim.

"A waiter," I repeated. "Is he connected to anyone who worked at the investment firm?"

Barbie settled into the chair at the desk. "That's the kind of detail we need to research."

"And we need to know all there is to know about Chet Kowalski. Address, marital status, where he worked, where he was killed ... all of it."

For once it was surprisingly easy to come by the information we wanted. Mostly this came down to the twins, Peggy and Pearl. Their contacts at the IRS office where they formerly worked – they'd only retired in the summer – could not be more happy to run background checks for them. I got the impression the fierce old ladies were something of a legend back home.

Chet Kowalski lived in Brooklyn with a girlfriend called Linda Travers. He worked at a Starbucks a two-minute walk from his address and was killed right next to it. He died from a single shot to the chest, his body left to go cold just out of sight of the street inside the entrance of an underground parking lot.

There was no visible link to Houston Investments that any of us could find so we were going to have to do things the old-fashioned way – by asking people.

Molly, Anders, Schneider, and Sam were going to track down and speak to as many of Houston Investment's former employees as possible. I wanted to know why the firm shut down so abruptly. Were they cyber hacked? If so there had to be more to it than that. Like why did the thief not take all the money from all their investors? The interviews would have to be conducted in person – over the phone, they would just get hung up on. The team could also question whether any of them knew Chet Kowalski.

Barbie was coming with Jermaine and me as we went to visit the murder scene and then Chet's girlfriend. My money was on her as the person most likely to give us the answers. Surely, she would know what he was doing inside an abandoned office yesterday and why he was being attacked.

That just left Gloria's Gang.

The Girlfriend

- -

Try as I might, there was no way to convince the older ladies to sit on the side-lines. To be clear, I wasn't trying to leave them behind because I thought they couldn't keep up or had nothing to offer, but because they are barmy and unpredictable. Two of them produced taser guns yesterday for heavens sake. What would they do next?

Accepting the inevitable with a smile, I made sure everyone was ready, gave Anna and Georgie to Alistair to have in his private quarters for the day, and headed down through the ship to the exit.

Our first stop was at the crime scene just off East 32nd Street. We only knew the location because the newspaper showed the front façade of the underground parking lot.

The crime scene people were long gone and there was very little left to show anything might have happened the previous evening. Not so much as a blood stain marred the concrete though a few loose ends of police barrier tape were visible where it had been tied to a lamppost.

There wasn't a whole lot to see.

Moving on, we walked to Chet's apartment. His girlfriend would know about his death and my expectation was that she would either be there or with friends. To track her down

I figured I might need to ask her neighbours where she worked and from there, via several phone calls, find out who she was staying with.

I had to do none of that because she was home.

"H-hello?" she answered the buzzer.

"Good morning," I like to start with a polite and friendly introduction. "My name is Patricia Fisher, am I speaking with Linda Travers?"

"Are you a reporter? I've got nothing to say to you. Please leave me alone!" The voice carried a tearful tone and was breaking as she shouted her final demand.

I pressed the buzzer again and again, attempting to explain who I am, but got no response. That could have been the end of it, but one of the building's residents chose that moment to exit and Jermaine was swift enough to catch the door before it closed again.

The elevator could only fit one of the mobility scooters and Linda lived on the fifth floor. I thought that was going to cause a big delay, but Gloria's Gang all elected to leave their scooters behind. Parking them in a corner and taking their keys, they joined the rest of us in the elevator.

"It's a bit of a squeeze," remarked Barbie who was squashed between Peggy and Pearl.

Spilling onto the fifth floor a few moments later, we found the door for Linda's apartment just a few yards down a hallway to the left.

Jermaine knocked three times and stood back. Waiting for Linda to open it, I glanced to my right. There were footsteps echoing in the stairwell and they had just decided to exit onto the same floor as us.

It was only my natural curiosity that caused me to look their way, but the two men coming through the door from the stairwell aimed themselves in our direction only to change their minds. To me, it appeared as though they changed where they wanted to go only when they saw my group.

They walked away down the hall in the opposite direction, murmured conversation going back and forth between them. I was still watching when one checked over his shoulder to see if I was looking his way. When our eyes met, he quickly snapped his head back to look where he was going.

I thought his behaviour was odd, but Linda opened the door and that distracted me from giving it any further thought.

"We're not reporters," said Gloria, getting in first because I'd been watching the two men.

Linda was peering around the side of her door, a security chain still in place for the little protection it provided.

She said, "Okay. So what do you want?"

That she hadn't slammed the door already was a positive sign.

I tried to introduce myself again.

"I'm Patricia Fisher, Miss Travers. I was hoping to talk to you about what happened to Chet. My friends here saw him being attacked yesterday."

"That's right," said Gloria. "Saw the whole thing."

"You saw him get shot!" Linda blurted, panic filling her voice.

"Um, no," replied Gloria. "We saw him being strangled."

Linda's face, still peering at us around the edge of her door, creased with confusion.

"But he wasn't strangled. Someone shot him."

With a small sigh, I said, "I think this might be easier if you could let us in, Linda. The ladies," I indicated Gloria's Gang, "cannot stand for too long."

Linda frowned. "That's not my problem. I didn't ask you to come here. The cops are investigating Chet's murder. If you think you know something about the crime, go and talk to them." The door slammed shut to accentuate her advice.

Yelling through the door, Gloria said, "We already did! They didn't listen to us. We saw the killer. It might be someone you know!"

No answer came back.

Barbie skewed her lips to one side. "Did she seem unusually uncooperative to anyone else?"

I shrugged. "She's grieving. Emotions that strong can make people act irrationally. Also, she doesn't know us and we're on her doorstep unannounced and uninvited."

"Yes," Barbie argued, "but we just told her we can identify a man who was attacking her boyfriend mere hours before he was gunned down. She ought to want to help bring her boyfriend's killer to justice."

Her phone rang, the sound of it loud in the hallway. Traipsing back to the elevator, for there was no reason to linger, I could hear Barbie chatting with someone and her voice becoming excited.

Rather than all squeeze into the car to ride down again, I volunteered to take the stairs with Barbie and Jermaine.

Gloria's Gang took the elevator, the doors closing just as we went through the door to the stairwell.

Barbie ended her call with, "I'll be there as soon as I can," and touched my arm to make me stop. "You'll never believe who that was," she teased, her eyes alive with excitement.

I wanted to say something flippant or amusing, but my brain doesn't work like that. Instead, I shrugged.

Starting slowly down the stairs with Barbie a step behind me and Jermaine in front, I said, "Surprise me."

"The assistant curator guy from the museum. Yesterday he was all negative about the San José, suggesting our search would bear no fruit."

"And now?"

"Now he's only gone and found me some more artefacts and the diary of the captain of the San José!" she squealed with glee.

I grinned at her. "This curator is a guy, right?"

Jermaine fought to supress a snigger.

Barbie's giant blue eyes filled with question. "Yeah. Why?"

I tilted my head to one side in a 'Come on, Barbie,' pose. "Because of those," I nodded my head at her ample bosom.

Barbie looked down at her boobs and back up at me, a frown on her face.

"Can't it be because he sees me as a scholar and wants to provide a service to a fellow intellectual."

Jermaine snorted a laugh. "Oh, I'm sure he would like to provide a service."

Barbie's frown deepened and she stuck out her tongue. "Now you're just being crude. Well look, I'm going back to the museum unless you feel you need me here. This could be pivotal to our investigation."

"You should go," I agreed, all joking aside. "I hope it doesn't prove to be a wasted trip."

We had come to a pause halfway down the first flight of stairs to discuss Barbie's call and were about to get moving again when I saw two shadows pass by the frosted window behind her.

Barbie went by me, stopping to see what had my attention.

"What's wrong, Patty?"

I bit my lip. "Nothing. Probably." Giving her my attention, I said, "You should go. Send messages and stuff to tell us what you find."

We air-kissed on the stairs and she bounded away, high-fiving Jermaine when she passed him.

Jermaine started down the stairs again, but stopped when he realised I wasn't following.

"Madam?"

"Hmmm?"

"Madam, you appear to be staring at the door to the stairwell, do you wish to go back and reattempt your conversation with Miss Travers?"

I didn't answer straight away. I was listening.

"Debt collection," growled a man's voice. It was followed by a loud thump.

When the scream came a moment later, I was facing the right way, cursing that I was right, and jolly thankful I had Jermaine with me.

Debt Collectors

The shadow I saw going by was the two men acting shifty a few minutes ago. I knew that before I got back through the door and could see Linda's door was now open. There was no one in the hallway which meant they had to be inside her apartment.

Jermaine caught up to me just as I turned toward Linda's place.

"Madam, if you please," he insisted politely. What he meant was that I should stay out of the way until he'd done his thing. I was happy enough to do so because the duo of male voices coming from Linda's apartment were raised and angry and the thump we'd both heard had been one of them kicking the door open.

Nevertheless, I wasn't letting Jermaine get too far in front of me.

"Be careful, sweetie!" I begged as he ran through the open door.

Peering around his back, I could see one of the men had hold of Linda. She was fighting to get away, but had neither the strength nor the know-how to escape the man's clutches.

Jermaine took out one of Linda's assailants before either man realised the tall Jamaican was there. He moves fluidly when he needs to, his movements precise and destructive.

Approaching from behind, he stepped into the man's personal space and used his entire body weight to propel him across Linda's living room.

The second man jerked his head around to face the unexpected additional person. Giving Linda a rough shove he came into a fighting stance.

Linda's legs tangled, sending her to the carpet with a cry of pain.

The second man had short red hair and a beard with a spatter of white around the chin. He was maybe six feet and two inches tall, which made him just a bit shorter than Jermaine, but he had a brawler's build. The way he held himself, his arms and legs loose and ready to strike, gave me the impression he knew how to fight.

The first man was getting back to his feet, blood coming from his lip where he'd hit the floor hard. He was shorter and lighter than his companion but looked no less mean.

"Gentlemen, I advise you against your intended course of action. If you resist, I will be forced to thrash you."

Red looked at his pal, "What did he just say?"

Red's friend shrugged. "No idea. Some fancy words in a stupid accent." He pulled out a knife, making my heart flutter and drawing a squeal of fright. "How about I cut him open, and we see if smart-mouthed limeys in bowler hats bleed just like everyone else?"

Red produced a knife too and I wanted to scream for Jermaine to run. I would have done so if he hadn't then chosen to move so fast it took my breath away.

One second he was facing the two goons, his hands behind his back where they gripped his umbrella. The next thing I knew the brolly whipped around in a wide arc, moving so fast it made a 'zzzzz' sound cleaving the air in two.

The handle caught Red on the wrist, knocking the knife out of his hand with such force it flew across the room to embed itself in the wall where it stayed. The brolly didn't stop there though. Jermaine was airborne, flying toward his target holding the umbrella like it was a katana. Reversing the unusual weapon, he swung the tip up to strike Red under his chin.

Red's friend lunged with his knife, finding empty air when Jermaine nimbly ducked. Coming up beneath him as Red's friend overextended, Jermaine opened the umbrella into his face to stun him, then closed it again so fast my eyes could barely keep track. The handle hooked around the man's neck and now off balance, he pitched into Red, their heads colliding with a crack of skulls.

Sensing they were beaten, their next move was to run for the door. Or to put it another way, they ran straight at me.

Mercifully, they ran right by me as I hugged the wall. Careening into the hall, they turned hard left and kept running.

The sound of their feet on the stairs came as blessed relief.

Forcing myself to let go of the wall and prove my legs were still in working order, I hurried to Jermaine.

"Are you all right? Did they hurt you at all?"

Jermaine's attention was on his umbrella, two fingers poking through a hole in the material.

"They ruined my umbrella," he complained.

Reminding me that we were not alone, Linda asked, "Who are you people? How did he do all that ninja stuff? Why are you still here?"

These were all good questions and a nice prompt for me to begin getting the answers I wanted. First, though, I thought I ought to check if she was okay.

"Yeah, sure," Linda replied flippantly. "Guys break into my apartment demanding money all the time. This is just a regular week for me." She looked like she was handling it really well, but her face crumpled a moment later and a sob escaped.

Touching Jermaine's arm, I didn't need to say anything.

"I'll make some tea, madam."

Guiding Linda to a couch, I let her cry while I picked up some of the mess the fight created. By the time I was done, her sobs were subsiding.

"I'm sorry," she snivelled through her tears. "I'm ... it's all a bit much to take."

I sat next to her, my arm around her shoulders. "You poor thing. Is there anyone we can call for you? It doesn't do to face these things alone. A sister perhaps? Or your mum?"

She shook her head which dislodged a few more tears, the drops of salty water cascading to land on her jeans.

"No. There's no one. My mom is in Seattle. I have friends, but they are all working, and they don't need this in their life."

I wanted to argue; it really wasn't good to handle such overwhelming emotions without someone to give support.

"This is Jermaine," I introduced my tall butler when he returned bearing a tray of steaming mugs. "He's my friend and he's always there for me when I need him. Are you sure you don't have anyone we can call? I'm sure they will be only too happy to help."

"I said there was no one! Okay?" She went from silent to shouting in a heartbeat only to settle again before the echo of her outburst subsided.

My phone rang, and I handed it to Jermaine with imploring eyes. He stepped away a pace to answer it. Gloria's name was on the screen, and I knew why she was calling: when they got in the elevator, we were right behind her.

Hoping I might now be able to learn something that would help Linda get justice for her boyfriend, I approached the subject from a tangent.

I showed her my phone, the screen filled with a newspaper article I'd just pulled up.

"Linda, my name is Patricia Fisher," I reminded her. "I'm employed as a professional detective."

Linda's eyes widened as she took in the headline above my picture and her head shot around so she could look at me. The article was one that came out just after the God-mother story broke. It wasn't my first time in the papers, but it was one of the few times I got to be reflected in a good light with a decent photograph. It was significantly better than the time I saved the Maharaja and showed the world my big bottom when I fell off the stage at his coronation.

"Who were those men, Linda? What did they want from you?" I was imploring her to help me and showing her who I was to make her want to open up.

Her reply came out quiet, her voice barely more than a whisper. "They wanted money."

My right eyebrow twitched. Of course, I'd heard one of them shout, 'Debt collection' right before they kicked in her door.

"Do you owe them?" I questioned.

She shook her head, saying nothing, and I thought I was going to have to probe to get answers until she started talking a few seconds later.

"They said Chet borrowed money from them and it was already overdue." She gasped as a thought gripped her. "Do you think they killed him?"

Rather than respond to her question because I had no idea who they were or why Chet might have been killed, I begged, "Tell me exactly what they said, Linda. As much as you can remember."

Linda's focus was on her hands which were crossed in her lap where they clutched each other as though she might lose one if she ever let go.

She took a moment to consult her memory before speaking.

"The one with the red hair did all the talking. He said Chet borrowed ten thousand dollars, that it was overdue, and that interest was being applied daily. I have to pay them fifteen thousand by the end of the week or they ... well, they didn't get to say what would happen when I fail to pay because you busted in and scared them off. I think they plan to hurt me though. I should go to the cops, right?"

"Yes, Linda, you should definitely go to the cops. Give them the best description you can and please reconsider going somewhere else for a few days."

"But they will come back, won't they?" She looked at me with fearful eyes. "I mean, they won't just let it go, will they? Even if the cops catch them, it's probably not their money, is it? They're just the collection guys who hurt people when they don't pay."

She was astute enough to see the truth of it.

I tried to give her reason for hope. "That doesn't mean you cannot beat them. If Chet borrowed money, do you know what it might have been for?"

She looked sad when she shook her head.

"I didn't know anything about it until they came knocking."

"What might Chet have wanted the money for?" I continued to ask the same question in different ways. "Was he trying to invest?" This time I got a look that suggested I had gone mad. "Did he ever talk about stocks and shares or that he'd met an investment banker who could help him?"

"He worked at Starbucks," she pointed out. "He didn't have two pennies to rub together. Buying stocks is what rich people do."

Sticking with the concept, I said, "When my friends saw him being strangled, he was inside Houston Investments. It's a hedge fund firm in Manhattan." I chose not to mention that it had shut down. I could introduce that later if there was a reason to. "What might he have been doing there, Linda?"

I had her interest, at least. "Houston Investments?" she repeated what I said. "I've never heard of it." She looked thoughtful for a moment, the skin around her eyes tightening as she wrestled mentally with something. "Sorry, I don't know that name. If you'll forgive me, I have to say this feels like a red herring. I only have your word for it that Chet was where you said he was."

She was pushing back, and I got the sense that she wasn't far from asking us to leave again. Had we not stepped in to save her from the debt collectors, I'm sure she would have already done so.

"He worked as a barista, didn't he?" I tried a new approach.

Linda answered this time. "It was supposed to be temporary. He's an actor. Was an actor," she added quietly, a tear escaping her right eye to run down her cheek where it wobbled but did not drop. "He was really talented. He always said he would get his break. It just never came, and he kept going to auditions in between working shifts."

The sound of the old ladies arriving in the hallway outside prompted Jermaine to open the door. There really wasn't room for them in Linda's small apartment, but they shuffled in anyway.

"What a lovely place you have," said Gloria, being nice and very British. Changing tact without pausing for breath, she said, "I saw your boyfriend's killer yesterday."

Linda eyed her sceptically. "You said that earlier, but he wasn't strangled, he was shot."

"It could have been the same person," Gloria settled herself onto a chair in the corner of the room, the last available seat in the apartment from the look of it. "His first attempt didn't work, so the killer went after him again."

Linda said nothing. I thought Gloria had a point, but there were hours between the time they said they saw him being attacked and the murder – why didn't Chet go to the police or seek safe refuge if there was a killer after him?

Gloria pressed on. "He was a handsome man. Tall with broad shoulders and sandy brown hair cut short at the sides and long at the back ..."

"A mullet," supplied Jermaine.

"That's right," agreed Gloria. "I forgot the word for a moment there. He had a mullet, and his hair had a natural curl to it."

I'd been watching Linda's face to see if she might react to the description, and got to see when she twitched.

"You think you know this man?" I cut in. It could be a significant lead.

Linda's eyes twitched my way, locking on mine for less than half a second before finding her lap again.

"No. No, I don't think so."

I couldn't be certain, but it sounded like a lie.

"Are you sure, Linda," I pressed her to reveal anything she thought she might know. "Even if the police are only able to eliminate him from their enquiries it will help their investigation." Or mine, I chose not to say. "Is this someone you've seen hanging around? Or someone you think Chet might know?"

Linda shook her head. "No, I'm sorry," she murmured. "I don't know anyone who looks like that. I wish I could help you, but I think you were right about me needing to find a friend. I'm going to call a few of them and go stay with someone else for a few days. It will help to be out of this apartment."

I tried to re-engage her, but it soon felt like I was pestering a distraught victim. She was in shock from her boyfriend's murder and undoubtedly troubled by the unexpected debt collectors' attack inside her apartment. I was just glad we were able to scare them off.

At Linda's request, we vacated her apartment. Back out in the street, Gloria's Gang had questions.

Retaliation

R eed Woodhead surveyed the bruises his employee now sported. Gavin and Tony were far from the sharpest tools in the shed, but they were capable individuals who had never previously failed him.

Gavin chose to interrupt Reed's lunch preparation to bring him unpalatable news and it pleased him that he had a kitchen knife in his hand while he listened to what Gavin had to say. The knife was for cutting cheese which he was going to employ in a grilled cheese sandwich, but was also doing a fine job of silently intimidating Reed's employee.

Reed noted how often Gavin's eyes would flick to his right hand where he held the knife in a nonchalant, yet poised manner.

"You say this is the work of one man?" Reed found himself questioning what kind of person could overpower two of his best enforcers.

For their part, Gavin and Tony had discussed the concept of lying to their boss and dismissed the notion. Getting beaten up by an Englishman wearing a bowler hat was embarrassing. Far better to agree it was a gang, but failing to return with the money was going to generate a reaction that would result in Linda Travers being questioned.

Basically, there was too much chance the truth would come out and their boss would believe her version over theirs since he would ask her questions using a pair of pliers.

"Yes, boss," said Gavin, nodding his head obediently.

"So, Miss Travers chose to hire someone to dissuade me from collecting that which I am owed," he concluded. It came as a surprise when Gavin challenged his assumption.

"Um, I don't think that's the case, boss." Now in the crosshairs of his boss's gaze, Gavin swallowed nervously and pressed on. "Um, what I mean boss, is that they weren't there when we arrived. Tony and I went to collect as instructed, but they arrived ..."

Reed held up an index finger, interrupting politely. "They? You told me it was one man."

"Um, yes, boss, but he had an older woman with him. She stayed out of the way and watched. He did all the damage like he was some kind of ninja."

Reed frowned, his sceptical look enough to close Gavin's mouth.

"And where is Tony?" he asked.

"Um, he's tailing them, boss. I ... that is, we thought you might want to know who they are and what else they are up to. Someone with an enforcer like that ... I mean, what if they are trying to muscle in on our ... I mean your, turf?"

Reed was impressed. Not that he showed it. Gavin and Tony spotted an angle that was yet to occur to him. What if the woman was trying to muscle in. The first thing Reed did when he set out to take over the money lending operation in Brooklyn was to find the opposition and remove them from the playing board. He recruited some of the old firm's men when the Alliance of Families fell apart and the rest became landfill or were bright enough to leave the city.

His mind now whirring, Reed said, "Get hold of Tony, find out where they are now, and tell him he'd better not lose sight of them."

Gavin had his phone in his hand before his boss finished talking, but paused to ask, "What are we going to do, boss?"

Reed stabbed his kitchen knife into the wooden butcher's block next to the chunk of cheddar – his lunch was going to have to wait. With the blade still quivering, he said,

"Retaliate. No one moves in on my turf. I'm calling everyone off their collections until this matter is resolved."

Gavin knew what that meant. It was a dog-eat-dog world in which they operated. It was the chief reason why none of the crew ever went anywhere alone – there were just too many new players around looking for a piece of the pie.

A grin curled the corners of Gavin's mouth as he dialled Tony's number and thought about catching up with the big guy in the stupid bowler hat.

Everyone is Missing

"**S**o what's next?" Peggy asked as spokesperson for Gloria's Gang.

There were several tasks on my to-do list, but first up was to check in with the other teams.

I called Schneider since he was the oldest and more naturally inclined to take charge in a passive, collaborative manner.

The Austrian answered with, "Patricia," which pleased me because it had taken a long time to get my team of security officers to relax. I was the only member of the ship's crew without a rank, and though it had been agreed I was to be considered equivalent to a Commander – which put me one step above the most senior member of my team, Lieutenant Commander Martin Baker – I was not about to have people salute me and constantly address me as ma'am. "I was just about to call you."

"Oh? You have something to report?"

"You could say that?"

I tried to guess what it was. "The former employees at Houston Investments are all pointing their fingers at each other and claiming they had nothing to do with the cyber hack that caused the firm to shut down."

"Not exactly."

I listened, staying quiet so Schneider could update me with his knowledge.

"They are all missing."

I blinked, my brain processing the news while the back of my skull itched feverishly.

"Missing. Like not at home? Or missing like kidnapped by aliens." I was half joking.

"The latter, though I doubt it was aliens." Before I could try to clarify his statement, he said, "Honestly, I'm not sure what to make of it. Speaking with a few neighbours, the reports are generally that they were there one day and gone the next. It's not just the former employees though, it's the whole family. Well, those who had a family or spouse. The apartments and houses are all empty and no one is answering their phones. We even got a couple of numbers for the wife/husband of the person working at Houston Investments and they're not answering either."

Reminding myself how the office looked to have been abandoned so fast everyone left their personal belongings behind, their further disappearance matched. It was bizarre and troubling news, and I had no idea what it could mean.

"And it's all of them?" I questioned.

"So far, yes. We have a couple of leads still to explore." Before I could question what that meant, Schneider supplied the answer. "At the last place we visited, the neighbour said he saw them leave in their car. Apparently, the husband – it's his wife who works for the firm – one moment." I had to wait for Schneider to consult his notes. "Rose Tyler is her name, senior VP of something or other. Anyway, the husband said they were heading to their lodge for a vacation, but the neighbour said they weren't packed right."

My brow wrinkled. "What does that mean? Not packed right?"

"The husband's fishing gear was still in his garage. So too the kayaks which they normally strap to the top of their car's luggage rack. I don't know where they might have gone, but they left in a hurry. We're going to keep looking unless you want us to stop."

The more I learned about Houston Investments, the more I wanted to know what was going on. I had a dead man, an abandoned office, a firm's worth of employees all taking to the hills or otherwise going missing, and debt collectors after money from the dead man who were willing to intimidate (or worse) the victim's girlfriend.

"Please stay on it, Schneider. The key to this might very well be in finding someone from that firm who can answer just a few basic questions." *Starting with: what the heck is going on?*

The call ended, I tucked my phone back into my handbag and faced my companions to give them an update.

They'd caught the gist of the conversation from hearing my half and were just as surprised as me to find out the hedge fund management firm were all on the run.

"If we assume they got robbed," said Pearl while looking like she wanted to scratch her head. "Why would they need to run away?"

Gloria snapped her fingers. "Because they stole the money!" She clapped her hands together in triumph.

"Ooh," said Peggy, "she might be on to something there."

I bared my teeth, trying to make Gloria's idea fit and straining my face while I did in what I had to guess was an unattractive way.

"Maybe," I acknowledged, not wanting to shoot Gloria's concept down without giving it proper consideration. "However, I would have thought that if they were going to steal the money, they would have done it in such a way that they were not under scrutiny."

"Maybe something went wrong," Gloria countered. "They planned it all perfectly, but a freak event scuppered their clean getaway, and they knew they had to get out before they got caught."

Once again, I didn't want to just poo-poo her notion and I wondered how much money their firms total pot might be worth.

"Jermaine, how many employees were there at Houston Investments?" I thought about how many desks I saw.

Jermaine had his phone in his hands, consulting the firm's website no doubt. Without looking up, he said, "It doesn't say, madam."

That didn't matter. "I saw a bunch of desks there. Maybe more than thirty. Hedge fund managers earn a lot of money so they would need to steal a whole lot of it to make it worth their while and it wouldn't be easy to create a conspiracy that included everyone in the firm." Not only that, I continued to reason even after I stopped talking, the *Wall Street Journal* article claimed there were only rumours of a cyber hack. The investors all had their money still.

Gloria wasn't letting go of her idea.

"Like I said: the plan went wrong. They only got a portion of what they were shooting for, but had to split because they knew they would get caught if they stayed."

I let the subject drop. Gloria had it wrong, but I had nothing concrete to prove that was the case. It just didn't feel … right. It failed to explain Chet's death for a start.

Sucking in a deep breath through my nose, I said, "I think perhaps we ought to pay Shanice another visit."

Vanished

A rriving back at the Roosevelt Building, I expected to find Shanice at the reception desk just like yesterday. In the cab on the way from Brooklyn, it had occurred to me that she might have the day off or work a split shift with someone else, but today the desk was simply unmanned.

The back of my skull itched the moment I realised she wasn't here, and a sense of unease crept up my spine when Jermaine caught my attention.

"Madam, there is a half-finished cup of coffee here."

I peered where he was looking.

"It's still warm," he reported, holding his finger against the outside of the mug.

I was about to ask someone to check the ladies' restroom, but Peggy was ahead of me, trundling her mobility scooter in that direction before I could speak.

Shanice wasn't there though.

There was no handbag or coat left behind, so she'd had time to gather her things before leaving. That felt positive, but wasn't exactly a relief.

The phone of her desk rang, jolting me with its abruptness. Jermaine flicked his eyes my way, asking if he should answer it.

I replied, "Let it go to voicemail," then wondered if it would. It didn't, and a few seconds after the call cut off it started ringing again.

With the reception abandoned, we could go where we wanted, but was there anything to gain from seeing the Houston Investment offices again? I hadn't found anything of worth last time. Also, I worried Shanice might be in trouble. Unlike the people working at Houston Investments, she hadn't run away, so perhaps whatever or whoever was behind their disbursement had returned to ask questions of the one person who might know.

I recalled reading an Agatha Christie book where the one person who knew what was going on in the house was the housemaid. My own maid, Molly, had come and gone about her business without comment or announcement. She would have known what was going on and have a head full of secrets.

Just like that, Shanice was the one constant who saw everyone come and go. She would know who worked there and who was just visiting. Not only that, she kept a log!

The thought crashed through my brain like a runaway train, and I ran around the desk.

Jermaine stepped out of my way with an expression that would have been quizzical if he were not so polite.

Landing in front of Shanice's computer, I stared at it for five seconds before getting up again.

"Jermaine, dear, can you please access the visitors' log?"

His eyebrows twitched, but he said, "I can certainly try, madam."

The computer hadn't been shut down and Shanice left so recently that the screen was yet to time out, so Jermaine didn't even need to enter a password. That she left so soon before we arrived sent a shiver down my spine.

Jermaine had the mouse in his right hand, clicking it sporadically as he navigated around the unfamiliar system.

"I think this is it," he said, sounding like he was talking to himself. Tearing his eyes from the screen, he looked around the wide desk. "I need a ..."

He didn't say what it was he wanted, but began rummaging through the things on the desk. Plucking one of those finger-sized data drives from the detritus of Shanice's drawer, he pushed it into a USB port, clicked the mouse a few more times, and sat back to watch.

I could not have done what he had, but I understood enough to know what just happened: he was sending the data from the visitors' log to the data drive so we could take it with us.

"I assume, madam, that you would rather move on than hang around here?"

"Very much," I agreed.

He popped the data drive out and into the inner jacket pocket of his immaculate suit.

"What are we doing?" asked Gloria. "Did Jermaine find something?"

"Possibly," I replied, hitching my handbag back onto my shoulder. "We won't know until we get to analyse it later. Shanice's absence is troubling. I think we ought to visit her next."

Gloria's face became a grimace. "Yeah, we should visit her next. She was lying yesterday. Maybe beating the truth out of her will move things along."

I closed my eyes for a moment and thought about massaging my temples.

"You can't just beat people to get them to give you information, Gloria."

"Well, duh. I'm too old for all that. I was going to get Jermaine to do it."

Jermaine's eyebrows took a hike up his forehead.

"I hear he's great at hitting people," Gloria concluded gleefully. Clearly, she relished the chance to make Shanice tell the truth.

Firmly, and leaving no room to manoeuvre, I stated, "No one is beating information out of anyone."

Gloria gave me a look that suggested I was being ridiculous.

Jermaine rose from the reception desk chair.

"How will we find where she lives, madam?"

"I can find her address," volunteered Peggy, getting ready to engage her IRS contacts again.

I was already heading for the exit. "No need," I called over my shoulder.

The ladies were still on their scooters, all three zipping along to catch up. Jermaine got caught behind the traffic and was last to exit, by which time Gloria, who was next out after me, was quizzing me on how I knew where to find Shanice.

Grinning, I pulled a folded piece of paper from my handbag.

"There was a bill on her desk." I unfolded the paper to show them what it was. At the top of the utility bill, Shanice's address was going to lead us right to her.

If she went home, that is. My gut insisted she was somehow embroiled in whatever was going on at Houston Investments to the point that I prayed she had chosen to run away like the employees there had. Why she'd waited three days and then chosen to vanish, I could not fathom, but it was better that than she'd waited too long, and her rushed departure was in the boot of someone's car.

We took another trip across town, this time using the metro because traffic on the streets looked awful.

Shanice had a place in Queens in an apartment that overlooked a Home Depot store. Viewing the street, I tried to imagine what it must be like for her to work in a building filled with investment bankers making huge wages only to come home to her ratty neighbourhood. There wasn't a tree in sight, but there was plenty of litter.

One of the drawbacks to living on a cruise ship and travelling around the world is that you get used to everything being lovely and neat. You won't find so much as a piece of dropped chewing gum on the deck of the Aurelia and the ship only stops in the nicest ports. Places like Mogadishu are not on the approved list of destinations.

The overall effect is to create something of a shockwave when the passengers are returned to the harsh reality that litter and dirt exist.

Shanice's apartment was on the third floor and mercifully the elevator worked. Jermaine and I took the stairs while Gloria's Gang crammed into the steel box to ascend.

My thighs were burning by the time I'd finished climbing, Barbie's gym instructor voice echoing from the recesses of my mind that I should run down the stairs and do another three sets.

Ignoring that deplorable thought, I scanned the doors to find the right one.

The elevator doors swished open without a ping to announce its arrival, the ladies grumbling as they reversed out into the narrow hall as we were passing.

"It should be this way," I pointed.

You know those moments in life when you realise something is really amiss and your stomach does a little backflip thing to make you feel sick? Well, that's precisely what happened when I got to Shanice's door and found the keys in the lock.

"Madam," warned Jermaine, needing no other words to insist he was going in first.

"She left her keys in the lock?" questioned Pearl. "That's not clever."

I turned the key to open the door and called out, "Shanice? Shanice, are you home?"

No answer came back, the silence ratcheting my nerves up another notch.

Jermaine asked me to move to the side and went by me and into the apartment to check it before the rest of us ventured inside.

I hovered in the doorway, trying to breathe through my mouth and not hyperventilate while I waited for Jermaine to tell me he'd found Shanice ... in pieces.

"There's no one here," he announced, his voice coming from somewhere I couldn't see until he came back into view a moment later. "However, the apartment is wrecked. I would hazard that someone came looking for something and they either didn't find it or it was in the very last place they looked."

Now that was curious. She vanished at speed from her place of work, and we found her apartment unlocked. My instant reaction was to assume someone took her from the Roosevelt Building under duress and brought her back here to look for something.

"Are her drawers empty?" I asked. "Has she packed?" I added for clarification, just in case Jermaine thought I meant her kitchen drawers.

He didn't know but went to check while the rest of us filed inside her abode. I felt like an intruder because I was, but didn't let it bother me too much. Shanice lied about there being people inside Houston Investments yesterday. She might have had good reason to do so and was certainly under no obligation to tell me anything.

However, now she was missing, and I couldn't help but wonder if her current situation could have been avoided.

Peggy asked, "Do we call the cops? I mean, I'm not enthralled by the prospect of another conversation with Captain Danvers, but what if Shanice is in real trouble? We should tell someone, right?"

I gave that a little thought. On the one hand, if Shanice *had* been taken then the police needed to get involved and perhaps they would uncover what transpired at Houston Investments. On the other hand I had nothing to tell them.

A woman wasn't at her place of work when she should be – not a crime. She also wasn't at home and her keys were in the lock – still not a crime. There was no blood at either location and no suggestion of recent violence. The place looked to have been tossed, but equally it could be the case that Shanice was just a messy person who habitually left her clothes on the floor.

Jermaine came back into the room. "Her wardrobes appear to be untouched, madam."

Now there was reason to doubt she chose to make for the hills as the employees of Houston Investments seemed to have done. What did that leave?

Nothing good.

My phone rang to send a spasm through my heart just as it did the last time. It was Schneider calling again.

"We found one," he told me before I could even speak. "Benny Crozier's neighbour had a number for his sister. They used to date, apparently. That's Benny's sister and the neighbour, not Benny and his sister."

"Yes, yes," I cut in, a little impatient for information. "Did you manage to speak to him?"

"Not yet, but we spoke to his sister. She lives in Buffalo and Mr Crozier is staying with her. He showed up out of the blue two nights ago. She said he hadn't even packed and was still wearing his suit from work."

My heart thumped in my chest, my pulse reacting to what sounded like panicked citizens attempting to flee an apocalypse.

"Is he still there? Can she get him on the phone?"

"She wouldn't give me his number and said he had gone into town. She expects him back any time and promised to let him know I called. Don't worry, I'll be calling her back to chase that up. How is it going at your end?"

I huffed out a frustrated sigh before saying, "Not very well. Something very sinister happened at Houston Investments but I have no idea what it was. A cyber hacking explains the failure of the business, but would it really have folded so quickly. I ..." I stopped talking. I'd been about to question whose money the firm lost and only at that precise moment did it occur to me how pertinent that question could be.

"Patricia?" Schneider's voice echoed in my ear.

"Sorry. I've got to check something. I'll call you back. Please keep trying to find someone who worked at Houston Investments." I wished him luck and ended the call.

"What do we do about the police?" asked Peggy, still thinking we ought to report Shanice's absence.

"We've got nothing to tell them. They won't start an investigation into her whereabouts without probable reason to believe she might have come to some harm."

Peggy was going to argue when her sister started squawking and shouting.

"It's him! It's him! Girls look at this!"

Clutched in her hands, a photo frame was moving too fast for anyone's eyes to see what had her so excited. That is until she shoved it under Gloria's nose.

Ready to Kill

"They went in there?" Reed asked.

"Dat's right, boss." Tony felt quite proud to have tailed the group across New York from Brooklyn to Manhattan, and then across to Queens without losing them or allowing them to spot him. He'd bought a Statue of Liberty hat from a street hawker, slapping a twenty into the man's hand and getting no change as he hurried onward to avoid losing sight of his quarry.

The hat didn't help him to blend in, but changed his features until he was able to discard it a short while later and don a ballcap from a different stallholder. Together with a five-dollar pair of sunglasses, he managed to avoid being spotted for more than an hour.

His boss, Reed, kept wanting their location, but each time he gave it, the women and the man in the bowler hat set off again.

Finally, just when Reed was beginning to grow impatient, Tony got to report where they were and bring the gang to his location. Hanging out in front of the Home Depot, Reed's enforcers acted like shoppers, some holding trolleys to make them look like they were about to go in while they waited and watched.

The dame and the guy in the bowler hat spoke with English accents according to his two nitwit employees. That being the case, she probably didn't live in the apartment building they were watching and would come out soon enough.

When they did, Reed's men would strike.

The news that the woman, who Reed took to be the boss if the bowler hat was the enforcer, travelled with three decrepit old ladies was confusing, but Reed figured they were part of a con or a ruse of some kind. No one would suspect old ladies of being involved in organised crime which made it a genius strategy on the part of whoever this new player was, and one Reed was going to employ the moment he could figure out how.

Reed would ascertain who they were and how many were in their operation. After that, their bodies would be found in a dumpster - just another New York statistic.

Had Reed looked around ... indeed if any of his men had looked around with great intent and scrutiny, they would still have failed to spot the other man watching Shanice's apartment building. It would not be their fault though for the man was invisible.

Not like the Invisible Man, but in the manner of someone who went out of their way to never be seen.

Five storeys up, Alan Valdez had an excellent view of the street and the entrance to the building into which he'd watched Patricia Fisher disappear. Setting up his rifle, he felt little emotion about what he was about to do.

The price to eliminate the English sleuth exceeded his usual fee, half of which was already in his account. His client, an underling in a prominent organisation for whom he'd been contracted before, was willing to pay for a rush job – it had to be today.

Finding her in a city the size of New York ought to have been testing to say the least, yet given the Roosevelt Building as a starting point, for that was where his client knew she had been, Alan was amazed to see her coming out of it a day after she was reported to have left.

Why she chose to return was of no concern. Opting to follow, he noted an idiot wearing a ballcap and sunglasses also tailing Mrs Fisher's group. He could have made his move earlier, but Alan was nothing if not cautious.

He watched and waited, determining quite quickly that the man in the sunglasses also intended harm upon his target and that just wouldn't do. You don't take the money if someone else does the work – that's just unethical.

Sunglasses man managed to stay with Mrs Fisher's party all the way to an apartment block in Queens where he chose to hang back – maybe he wasn't such an amateur after all – and was joined by more than a dozen other men.

Alan Valdez prepared to take his shot and waited, ever patient for the target to once again appear.

A Connection Finally

"Y ou're sure?" I asked for the second time, just because I needed to be absolutely certain.

Gloria rolled her eyes. "Listen to the words coming out of our mouths, Patricia. This is the killer!"

The man in the photograph, Shanice's arms around his shoulders, certainly had a mullet and fit the description they gave earlier.

Distracted by Schneider's phone call, I hadn't ventured much beyond the entrance to Shanice's apartment. Had I done so I would have noticed the two coffee cups on the drainer, the male items in the bathroom, the man's clothing in the closet ...

Like Linda, Shanice lived with her boyfriend and his photographs were all over the apartment. At least now we knew why she lied about there being someone in Houston Investments yesterday: her boyfriend was Chet's killer.

"Now do we call the police?" asked Peggy, her tone derisory.

It was the obvious thing to do, but would they listen? Captain Danvers made it quite clear he didn't want to hear from me again. They dismissed the notion the ladies saw anything from the roof of the tour bus and would need something stronger than a photograph and a woman who might or might not be missing to get them involved.

Furthermore, when he inevitably asked how we obtained the photograph, I predicted a volcanic response to discovering we had set foot inside Shanice's apartment.

I explained as much to the ladies.

"So, what?" Pearl defied me. "We just do nothing and let Mullet Man get away with it?"

I bit my lip so I wouldn't bite at her barb. "Not at all. We carefully examine this apartment for a start. There could be dozens of clues here. Finding out his name would be a good start." I flicked my eyes at Peggy and Pearl. "Then maybe you can use your contacts to find out where he works." I let that idea sink in.

"Yeah, okay," agreed Peggy. "I guess that makes sense."

We set to work, all five of us carefully looking in drawers and through the detritus strewn around the apartment. We examined pieces of paper, and generally nosed around. We all looked for a computer or laptop, but if they owned one, which surely they had to, it wasn't in their apartment.

It was Jermaine who made the breakthrough when he found a post-it note stuck to the refrigerator door.

"Madam," he called for my attention, his eyes on the sticky note which was now in his fingers. "I believe this may be of help."

Gloria, Peggy, and Pearl crowded around so we could all see it.

The note read:

Herbert's Quest Rehearsal

2 o'clock

Rothman Centre

See Sheila

There was a date on it too. Today's date. The back of my skull itched.

"You think that's where he is?" asked Peggy.

Pearl checked her watch. "It's just gone 2 o'clock."

I backed away, heading for the bedroom. "Hold on, I have to check on something." Flicking my eyes at Jermaine I mouthed 'Thank you' and said, "Can you find out where the Rothman Centre is, please?"

Returning from the bedroom, I had a pile of papers in my hand. Or one could accurately call them a script.

"I think he's an actor." My announcement got everyone's attention. "This was on his nightstand." I held up the script for everyone to see. The title on the front cover read 'Herbert's Quest'.

I'd never knowingly held a script before, but I knew what it was. Two dozen pages in, the corner of a page was turned down and a whole bunch of lines were highlighted. If I had it right, our mystery man with a mullet was playing *'Argumentative Man'*.

Jermaine said, "The Rothman Centre appears to be a theatre, madam. It is just a few blocks from here."

I pursed my lips, thinking for just a second. There was something about the fact that the man we wanted – scouring the apartment failed to turn up a piece of paper that would tell us his name – was an actor. Chet was an actor too according to his girlfriend. That created a connection between killer and victim, but why would two actors be messed up in the affairs of a hedge fund company who had just shut up shop after possibly being cyber hacked even though no money appeared to be missing, and why would the man with the mullet want to kill Chet?

All I had were questions. Answers were a non-existent commodity, and I wasn't going to get any standing where I was.

"I think we need to get over there."

Paid to Kill

Reed got the nod from Ross, the one man among his employees who didn't look like a wannabe professional wrestler. In fact, Ross looked more like an accountant, but Reed knew not to be fooled; Ross was probably the most ruthless and bloodthirsty of all his men.

He picked Ross to act as lookout in the apartment building because he knew the English woman and her companions would think nothing of it if they happened to spot him. Ross would wave and say, "Hello,' and pass them by as though he lived in the building.

None of that was necessary though. Ross popped his head around the building's front door, waved across the street to where Reed and the rest of the hastily assembled team were standing, and went back inside.

The message was clear: They were coming.

By the time the door opened to reveal the tall, black man in the bowler hat, Reed's men were surrounding the entrance.

Reed was ten feet back, surveying the field like a general and confident this would be an easy take. The instruction was to let them file out. If they attempted to turn around when they saw what was waiting for them outside, they would find Ross holding a gun to insist they keep going.

However, Reed's simple instructions were addressed at idiots.

Keen to even the score, Gavin made sure to be close to the door and threw a punch at a point six inches below the rim of the bowler hat the moment it exited the building. He expected the punch to land and intended to leave it at that.

Call it sixth sense, call it intuition, or simply look at the door to see there was a frosted panel just to the right through which Jermaine could see a shadowy shape move. The punch sailed by the side of the bowler hat and the next thing Gavin knew he was face down on the pavement wondering why his teeth felt loose.

For his part, Jermaine thought the shadowy figure was a person waiting to get inside and was about to apologise for being in the way when he saw the fist coming for his face. On reflex, he gripped, twisted, yanked, and then reversed direction all within the space of a second which was all the time he needed to assess what his eyes were telling him.

Reed heard the man in the bowler hat shout a warning to those behind him – namely his principal and the old ladies – before exploding outward in a melee of flying limbs and, bizarrely, an umbrella.

Three of Reed's men were tumbling away before anyone thought to pull a gun. They all carried them – that was just good form, but rarely were they shown in public during daylight because conversely that was bad form.

The bowler hat stopped fighting when it was clear to continue would result in his death.

Behind him, the door had swung shut. It opened again now, a woman in her mid-fifties exiting with her hands raised to shoulder height. The three old ladies coming out behind her did not have their hands raised because they needed them to steer their scooters.

Reed had never felt the need to 'off' an old lady before, but he wasn't going to lose any sleep over it.

"They tried to get back inside, boss," said Ross, exiting the building last.

Cars went by in the street and there were people coming and going from the Home Depot. A few paused to look when they noticed something was occurring, only to realise what they were witness to and opted to quickly vacate the area.

Reed didn't like how things had gone, but it was too late to do anything about that now. It was time to get them off the street, find out what they knew, and make them vanish. Chances were that someone had already called the cops, even in this neighbourhood, and that put him against a ticking clock.

"Move them," he barked. "Into the alley."

The Englishwoman looked surprisingly scared for a person trying to move in on a rival gang's turf; Reed expected her to be tougher and she looked nothing like he imagined. Reed expected a woman with a face like a bulldog and clothing suitable for shaking down 'customers', not a knee-length cashmere coat and boots that came up to meet them. She looked elegant or refined maybe. Not the kind of person he would consider a threat.

Too late now though.

His men were all around the tall, black man in the bowler hat. They'd seen what he was capable of and had guns pressed into his kidneys on both sides. The woman was being treated just as harshly, hustled toward the alley, and the three old ladies weren't having to steer their scooters because his men had taken over the controls.

Reed lifted his right foot to begin following when his ears detected an odd kind of 'puff' sound. A fine red mist filled the air to the right of the Englishwoman and tracking it with his eyes, Reed was looking the right way when one of his men dropped like a stone.

Everyone paused.

"Billy?" Dom, the man nearest to Billy, nudged his colleague's inert form with a toe. "He's bleeding," Dom announced, confused to find an expanding pool of blood making its way from Billy's head.

Reed's face tightened and he was about to say something when the 'puff' sound came again.

This time it was Dom who had a halo of red mist where his head used to be. He was on the ground next to Billy, a second pool of blood spreading outwards from his skull.

Storming forward, Reed barged his employees out of the way to get to the woman who was now white with fear.

Grabbing her shoulders, he shook her. "How are you doing that?" he shouted into her face.

The woman, who now had specks of blood on her beautiful coat, stared up into Reed's eyes.

"I'm not doing it, you idiot!" she squealed. "There's a sniper!"

Reed turned to look, placing his own head directly into the crosshairs of Alan's Barrett Mk M22 MRad sniper rifle. All Alan Valdez wanted was a half chance of seeing his target which had been constantly obscured by other people's heads since she left the building.

Shooting people he wasn't being paid to shoot was also bad form, but his little girl had a play date at the park and there was always a stack of hot mommies there. He needed to get this job over with so he could pick Sophie up from kindergarten and be ready to dazzle as the best dad. Single moms couldn't resist the doting dad figure.

Reed squinted into the row of buildings opposite. "Where?" he asked. As last words go it was far from famous, but like most people, he didn't know he was about to die.

Sensing what was about to happen, Patricia ducked and scurried. That placed her out of range for the spreading red mist that had once been Reed's cerebellum.

Seeing their boss drop finally proved to be enough motivation to get Tony, Gavin, and everyone else moving. They ran, spreading outwards from the three dead bodies at speed.

Alan attempted to track his target's movements and fired two more times when he thought he might hit her. In the confusion of bodies, one bullet dug into the wall and the other caught a shoulder, spinning a man the rest of the gang knew as two-tone for his monochromatic wardrobe in a circle.

Two-tone ran off clutching his wound which left Alan to grumble his annoyance. Patricia Fisher had made it to the alley being carried by the tall Jamaican. Unlike Reed, Alan Valdez knew exactly who the Englishwoman was and by extension could identify her butler. The three old ladies were of no consequence, but they were all in an alleyway now and out of his sight.

Muttering his frustration, Alan came out of his firing position and gathered his things. There wasn't time to set up in a different building and Patricia Fisher would surely have the common sense to run away now.

To fulfil his contract, keep the money, and make it to kindergarten to pick up Sophie on time, he needed to move to the other end of the building where he believed he would have a shot into the alleyway.

The alley was a dead end - it didn't go anywhere, so Patricia Fisher and her friends were going to have to come back out of it soon. If he was quick and lucky, this kill could still be saved.

Who Shot Them?

I was out of breath and scared half out of my mind when Jermaine lowered me back to the ground. The lack of oxygen in my lungs had nothing to do with exertion on my part for I'd barely run a step, and all to do with the horror of watching bodies drop all around me.

The inescapable message playing on loop in my head was that the sniper had been aiming at me.

Careening to a stop like a mobility scooter stunt display team, Gloria's Gang arrived by my feet.

"Here, what the heckity-heck was that all about?" asked Gloria.

Peggy and Pearl were likewise inclined to seek answers.

"Who were those guys?" asked Peggy.

"And what happened to them?" questioned Pearl.

Jermaine could see that I was wrestling with a distinct desire to vomit and was kind enough to supply answers on my behalf while I lowered my head to waist height and used the wall to stop myself from collapsing.

"We met two of those gentlemen earlier, ladies," he began. "They were in Miss Travers' apartment where they were hassling her for money her deceased boyfriend owed them."

"They're the ones you beat up?" Peggy sought confirmation.

In his typically understated fashion, Jermaine said, "I reinforced the idea that they ought to leave Miss Travers be. Since they returned with additional numbers, I feel it is safe to assume they were unhappy with how our encounter concluded."

Pearl managed to translate what my butler was trying to convey. "So they're a bunch of hoodlums running a loan shark racket among other things, and they came to get even for you showing them the door."

"Precisely."

"So who shot them?" asked Gloria.

I levered myself off the wall.

"That's not the important question right now."

"It's not?" questioned Peggy.

I shook my head, but not too vigorously because I still felt quite woozy.

"No. The important question is what are we still doing here? That sniper was aiming at me."

I got questioning looks from everyone.

"I mean, I think they were. It was the guys all around me that kept getting hit. Whatever. I don't think staying here is a good idea." Not least because there are dead bodies in the street.

Jermaine agreed, moving to position himself ahead of me as we moved back toward the mouth of the alley.

It wasn't far to the nearest Metro station, and I would be happy to run all the way if it got me there alive.

Of course, this is me we are talking about, so we were still heading back to the street when cars started to pull up ahead. People, or rather, men exited the cars almost before they stopped moving. The cars obscured our view of the street, and the men soon blocked the alleyway to ensure we couldn't leave.

"Here" said Gloria, "I recognise these fellas. They were in that mattress shop's loading bay yesterday arguing about drugs."

Oh, perfect.

Barbie and Hugo

- -

B arbie quite enjoyed being left alone to travel across the city. Sharing the day with Hideki would be nicer, but he had to work, and she wasn't about to complain about the demands of his role as a junior doctor.

The crisp, cold New York air nipped at the tips of her ears where she chose to wear her blonde hair pulled up into a tidy, functional ponytail. It was more practical like that for working in a gym and Barbie found she habitually set it that way even on days when she didn't need to.

Riding the Metro and hearing the all-too familiar names of the stations being called out filled her heart with romantic notions of what her life could have been if she'd chosen to pursue modelling or acting as her parents and friends suggested she should. Neither career was one she wanted, but the fantasy of life in such a vibrant city teased her, nevertheless.

Exiting three stops early so she could walk above ground and take in the sights and smells, she stopped to get a to-go coffee and a vegetable burrito from a vendor. The calories would power her through to dinner time and the caffeine would give her brain some zip.

Arriving at the museum, she was surprised to find assistant curator for maritime antiquities, Hugo Lockhart, waiting for her on the steps leading to the entrance.

"No need to buy a ticket today, Miss Berkeley ..."

"We agreed yesterday that you would call me Barbie," she shot the bookish man a broad smile.

He dipped his head to acknowledge her reminder. "Barbie, yes. This way please."

He led her past the entrance where visitors were queuing to get in and to a door labelled 'staff only'.

"Is this okay?" she asked. "There's no need to get into trouble for sneaking me in if that's what you are doing." Barbie thought about Jermaine and Patty and their half-joked insistence the assistant curator was more interested in her *assets* than her interest in his chosen field of expertise.

Hugo tilted his head as though he found her comment curious.

"Nothing of the sort, Barbie. I'm merely expediting your passage to the correct area. You are here under invitation today. Here," Hugo fished in his pocket for the thing he'd forgotten, "put this on."

Barbie turned the badge around. It had a small crocodile type clip on top so it could be attached to a person's clothing and displayed the words 'Official Visitor' in bold letters.

"Now, please follow me. The museum is set up for visitors to take a winding route through the halls, but we can cut across them to get to the private research room where the latest artefacts are set out and waiting for you."

Hugo chose not to mention that he was given strict instructions to make sure Barbie was not recorded coming through the museum's main entrance where there were cameras set up. Senor Silvestre wanted her to see the artefacts he provided and for Hugo to discuss them with her. Senor Silvestre wanted to hear what the blonde woman had to say, especially where it pertained to the possible location of the San José.

Hugo had wanted to argue that the San José had been sunk in 1708, but Senor Silvestre was paying too handsomely for Hugo to consider contradicting his beliefs. If the Spaniard wanted to invest in a crazy fairy tale, Hugo didn't care one bit.

Settling the attractive woman at a table, Hugo left the room to fetch refreshments. That was just an excuse though; he needed to let Senor Silvestre know the woman was with him.

Barbie stared down at the new artefacts. They were all interesting, but it was the captain's diary that got her most excited. The three-hundred-year-old document was displayed inside a glass box, a transcription and translation of its contents on a tablet to its right.

Licking her lips, she began to read.

Fish in a Barrel

O ur day was going from bad to worse and it really did feel like we had just escaped the frying pan only to land in the fire.

The men blocking our path were too many for Jermaine to stand a chance against, skilled fighter though he is. A deranged voice inside my head giggled that I should commission a range of exploding handbags for deployment when situations such as this one arise.

A rough count told me there were more than twenty men on the street, plus the drivers who were still in their cars. They wore suits without ties and could be mistaken for office workers on their lunchbreaks were it not for the menacing behaviour and the troubling fact that I knew they were involved in the illegal substances market.

There were no weapons on display, unlike the previous bunch, but I doubted they were unarmed.

Creating a sort of funnel, the men left a gap in the middle through which another man walked. That he was in charge was in no doubt and I'd seen him only the previous day, leading the argument about product and cashflow in the loading bay of the mattress shop.

"Boss, there are three bodies in the street," a man reported. "Looks like they just got shot."

"That's gonna draw the cops," said another of the lieutenants.

"Then we shall be brief," the boss replied without taking his eyes off me. "Your handy-work?" he asked.

I blinked, surprised at the question, and took a moment to respond because I wasn't certain my voice would work.

My delay prompted Gloria to offer her opinion. "Yeah, and guess who's going to be next, young man."

Her blind threat got me talking. "No, it wasn't us. I think there's a sniper in one of the buildings behind you."

Instantly, the gang of men jerked around to look at the buildings, eager eyes searching for any indication there might be danger present.

One of them came closer to the boss.

"We should take them and go," he advised.

I swallowed nervously. One might more accurately call it a gulp. Were my knees shaking? Adrenalin had surged through me when we left Shanice's apartment building to find ourselves surrounded by thugs. It went wild when the sniper started shooting, and just when it began to leave my bloodstream, which always leaves me feeling spent, these guys showed up.

The boss came to stand in the centre of the alley, his deep, dark brown eyes boring into mine. He stood a shade under six feet, with tan skin and features that made me think he was from a South American country. Brazil maybe. Or Columbia. I didn't know, but his flawless English carried an accent from his home nation. He was in his twenties, maybe not much older than twenty-five and now that I was paying attention, I noted the rest of his men looked to be about the same age. There was something very familiar about him. I couldn't put my finger on it, but I wanted to claim that I knew his face.

To me it felt that they were on the young side to be operating as an organised criminal gang. Was there an older boss somewhere pulling the strings?

The leader shook his head in response to his advisor's words. "This will only take a moment." Looking straight at me, he said, "You were at Houston Investments yesterday. Tell me where William Chalice and the rest of the staff have gone."

At least it was easy to return an honest answer.

"I have no idea where they are. I'm trying to find them myself."

The man narrowed his eyes a little.

"You expect me to believe that?"

"It's the truth," I assured the man. "I'd never heard of them before yesterday. I was only there because my friend thought they saw someone being murdered."

"We did see someone being murdered," Peggy insisted.

"Who?" the man asked. "Who was being murdered?"

How should I answer that? Wondering where the heck the cops were, I decided to go with the most honest response I could give.

"Well, he wasn't actually killed there. He was killed later. The ladies saw him being strangled but he was killed later when someone shot him. His name was Chet Kowalski ..." I was babbling, and in so doing I managed to aggravate the person I hoped to keep calm.

"I do not advise testing my patience," he growled.

"Boss?" The men were becoming agitated, and a siren had just sounded in the distance. It was a couple of blocks away, no more. "Boss, we need to leave this area before the cops turn up and assume those bodies are to do with us. Let's take the Brits with us and ..."

"Sure," the boss snapped. "Put them in the cars."

The boss's trusted lieutenant whistled and six of the gang peeled off to come our way. The siren was joined by another as multiple units converged. The men moved fast, coming right for us. Next to me, Jermaine tensed, and I feared for what would happen when one of the gang grabbed me and my butler made them eat their own elbows.

I had no desire to be taken anywhere - I've been stuffed into the boot of a car before and can report that it is not a fun experience. However, as the men closed the distance, blocking the alley with their bodies, I heard the all-too familiar sound of an automatic handgun being cocked.

I was facing the gang members and none of them were holding guns which meant ...

The deafening sound of guns being discharged in a narrow space filled my head like someone trying to fit more into a waste receptacle than it could hold and using a boot to stamp it down. My headache was instant. So too the knicker-wetting fear of getting shot by one of the insane gun-toting grannies to my rear.

Jermaine threw himself to the ground, his reflexes far faster than mine. I didn't have to move though, because he rugby tackled me on his way.

Still facing the boss and his gang members even though my face was flying toward the ground, I got to see four or five of them get hit. Confined by the walls of the buildings to either side, it really was like shooting fish in a barrel.

The shooting stopped, but by then the gang was in full retreat, the wounded being dragged along by those who had so far managed to avoid being shot.

"Oh, I'm out of bullets," Gloria complained.

"Me too," moaned Peggy.

"I said we needed to buy spare clips," said Pearl in a 'told-you-so' tone.

My heart hammered away, beating so fast I had to question if it was going to simply explode from my chest like something from an *Aliens* movie.

The sirens were closer than ever, and it seemed both incredible and impossible that it couldn't have been more than about two minutes since the sniper fired his first shot.

The gang's cars began to pull away, their tyres kicking up dust and grit as they powered away from the kerb.

Just like that, we were alone again.

Back on his feet, Jermaine got to me before my legs buckled.

"Are you all right, madam?" he asked, his voice soft.

A giggle escaped my lips. "Am I all right?" I giggled again, but this time the deranged amusement was shunted to one side by a stronger emotion: anger.

Spinning about to glare at Gloria's Gang, I shouted, "Where did you get the guns? It's bad enough that you almost got us all killed yesterday with your stupid tasers. Today you thought it would be a good idea to level up?!" I was in full rant mode. "What were you thinking? You just shot half a dozen people!" Peggy tried to talk and got drowned out as my rage continued. "What's next? Bazookas?

Peggy and Pearl exchanged a glance – I'd just given them an idea.

"You're all going straight back to the ship! I'm confining you to the ship!"

"Can she do that?" Pearl asked her twin sister.

"I can do whatever I want! I'm the ship's detective!" I couldn't do any such thing, but my brain had taken a detour and missed its stop at the station called 'rational'. "I must have been out of my mind to get involved in your crazy murder enquiry! I could be sipping gin at the top of the Empire State Building, or having a day at the spa!"

The sound of a car skidding to a halt in the street beyond the alley we still hadn't left, cut through my thoughts. I knew it had to be the police, but a portion of my brain insisted I needed to check for myself just in case it was yet another gang of psychos come to end my life.

It *was* the cops; I could see the nose of their squad car, but they weren't checking the alley. There were bodies in the street, and they probably didn't know we were in here.

Having lost my train of thought, the emotions swirling around my head overwhelmed me. A sob jerked my body as I fought against tears that wanted to come. Jermaine's hand on my shoulder was the last straw.

He was giving me his support, his strength, and I folded into his chest like a damp tissue, my face leaking into his cotton shirt.

"Does she often do this?" asked Pearl.

Gloria said, "Never seen it before. I think it's the two of you having this effect. I've never made her cry."

Complaining, Peggy said, "You'd think she'd be grateful we bought the guns. Where would she be now if we hadn't started shooting?"

Tucked inside Jermaine's strong arms, I could hear what they were saying. They were right, of course, and that made things worse. I would apologise for shouting once I thought I could control my voice. It was going to have to wait a while though because the cops had just found us.

Clarification Required

Alan Valdez slipped quietly through a back door one street over from the events outside Shanice's apartment building. The sniper rifle, broken down and stored neatly away inside a case designed to look like a toolbox, went into the back of a van displaying the livery of a plumbing company.

The livery would be gone an hour from now, replaced with something new. That was just a routine part of his work and went along with cleaning and storing his rifle and other tools inside a secure lockup close to the river.

None of those routine tasks came into his mind though.

He'd accepted a contract and had failed to fulfil it. By choice. There had been a couple of instances in the past where circumstance denied him a kill, but he could not remember choosing not to pull the trigger ever before today.

Not that he elected to spare the life of Patricia Fisher, she had nothing to do with it. Not directly at least. It was the people she was talking to in the alley that gave him pause.

Manolo Ravassa was the son of the head of the Columbian cartel. Alan knew this because Manolo's father, Juan Pablo Ravassa, had hired him many times in the past. He also knew the ageing patriarch, Hector Luis Ravassa, Juan Pablo's father, died just a few months ago and that the Columbians moved into New York in the wake of the Alliance of Families disintegrating.

Ironically, Patricia Fisher was the woman responsible for that, but seeing her conversing with Manolo, who Alan knew was here to run and develop the New York operation, generated more than a few questions.

He could have pulled the trigger and got paid, but the very fact that his target was talking to Manolo threw the legitimacy of his contract into doubt. The man who called him gave Alan reason to believe the order for the hit and the payment for it came from Manolo Ravassa and that was clearly not the case.

There would be other opportunities to kill Patricia Fisher if that was what his client still wanted. However, Alan wanted clarification before pulling the trigger. It wasn't like it was something he could undo afterwards. He also needed to collect Sophie from school and flirt with some hot mommies and that was next on his list; clarification could wait until after that.

Stress-induced Ulcer

The cops sat me down with a sweet cup of coffee, letting me recover while they dealt with the bodies in the street and quizzed Gloria's Gang about their weapons.

I would have answered questions too, but my sobbing fit left me with that ridiculous after effect where you keep snivelling for half an hour and struggle to speak or make sense.

The old ladies bought the handguns from some teenage boys on a street corner the previous evening just a few hours after having their tasers confiscated. It horrified me that they would even approach such unpredictable individuals, let alone hand over cash, but by their own admission, they went looking for them.

According to Peggy, "We can't run away at our age, so getting tooled up is the obvious alternative."

They smuggled the guns on and off the ship inside the seats of their scooters which get a basic search by the security team, but go around the metal detectors at the ship's entrance for obvious reasons.

It was something I would address with the ship's security team the moment I returned to the Aurelia. Who would have thought there was a need to search women in their eighties for automatic weapons?

There was nothing illegal about purchasing the weapons – Peggy and Pearl bought them because they had addresses in the US. Giving one to Gloria was dodgy ground and firing them in the street even dodgier, but it was easy to argue they were using them in self-defence.

The police confiscated the guns, nevertheless, however the ladies could collect them later provided they were going to be used for home defence. Since we were all getting back on the cruise ship, the guns would stay with the police and I, for one, was jolly glad about that.

The cops were able to identify one of the sniper's victims by sight. Reed Woodhead was a small-time hoodlum trying to make a name for himself. He'd been arrested many times before which was how the cops knew him. Officers went to look for the sniper, a little startled by the concept and very definitely worried it might be a vigilante behind the trigger.

I felt quite certain they were not going to find him. Or her, I conceded, remembering that in my group of friends, Deepa was the trained infantry sniper. Whoever it was, they didn't fire a shot after the one that killed Reed; a reasonable indication they were no longer in the area.

Captain Danvers appeared about half an hour after the first cops. By then the bodies were covered over and I was feeling more like my usual self. It was my insistence that caused the detectives to contact their boss.

"More bodies?" he shot me an unhappy look. Sighing, he said, "Of course there are more bodies. You leave a trail of them everywhere you go. Why don't we cut to the chase, and you tell me why I just dragged my butt across town?"

"We identified Chet Kowalski's killer," I stated bluntly. "He's the boyfriend of Shanice Garner, the receptionist at the Roosevelt building where the ladies," I indicated Gloria's Gang, "saw him strangling Chet yesterday."

"Told you, didn't we," spat Gloria, unhelpfully.

Trying to keep Captain Danvers' focus on me I said, "We believe he is at the Rothman Centre right now, acting a part in a play or a TV show or something."

"The Rothman Centre," Danvers repeated. "You think he's there right now."

"Yes."

"And you can identify him?"

"Yes."

Captains Danvers placed a hand on his gut, making me think he was suffering from indigestion or something. Given how stressed he looked, I had to wonder if his job had given him an ulcer. I could see he wasn't happy about it, but he couldn't ignore the possibility that I was right.

"You know this how?" he asked.

I squirmed a little. We had completely legitimate reasons for entering Shanice's apartment, but that didn't mean Captain Danvers was going to like it.

I could feel my face flinching away from his response even before I started to explain.

"You were in her apartment?" he checked that he understood what I was admitting to.

"Yes."

"All of you?"

"Yes."

"Nosing around?"

"Yup."

"Because you're still looking for Chet Kowalski's killer."

I cringed a little. "Yeahhh. We're really close now though. We know he borrowed money from the shady characters that ambushed us coming out of Shanice's apartment building."

"You mean the ones lying in the street with holes in their heads?" The police captain's voice sounded a little fried and was building to a crescendo. "The ones you appear to have led to their deaths?"

That felt a little harsh.

"You realise I have to explain all this to the chief, right? When you met him earlier, did it seem to you that he was a forgiving person?" He started to mutter, "I must need my head tested. All I had to do for an easy life was lock you up for a couple of days."

Interrupting just a little, I said, "We also know there really is something going on with Houston Investments. The men who cornered us in the alley," I referred to the gang who cleared out just before the cops arrived.

"The ones your elderly friends shot holes in?" Danvers now sounded like he might begin to insanely giggle if pushed much further.

"Yes," I agreed, unsure what else I could do. "They wanted to know where the staff from the investment firm are. They hoped I might know and were prepared to snatch us off the street to find out. They must be involved in the reason why my people cannot find anyone from Houston Investments. The entire firm have left the city and some of them did so without going home for a change of underwear. What does that tell you?"

"That you shouldn't have people looking into it?" Captain Danvers sighed and looked to the heavens. Before I could say another word, he held out his right arm with the index finger held aloft in a don't say anything gesture. "You think you know who killed Chet Kowalski and where they are right now?"

"Yes."

Danvers shook his head, muttering to himself.

We were all going to the Rothman Centre.

Master of Disguise

X avier Silvestre enjoyed disguises. He considered himself a master at changing his appearance. Today, he wore cowboy boots that were cleverly designed to provide an additional four inches of height. Growing from five feet eight inches to six feet tall altered the perception of all those who might see and remember him.

Tucked in his gum at the front of his mouth, a wad of chewing tobacco added another element to his disguise. A leather string tie, silver tips on the collar of his shirt, and a Stetson hat artificially aged so it wouldn't look new, were enough he believed, to convince anyone who didn't hear him speak, that he was an American.

He thought his outfit to be ridiculous simply for the stereotyping it cast, yet that was a good thing. People would see the outfit and not the man.

A wig on his head provided blonde hair that fell to his collar and glued to his face, a beard that hung six inches below his chin.

Unrecognisable, he thought to himself as he passed a mirror.

Just a few minutes earlier, he'd received a message from Hugo Lockhart to confirm the blonde woman, Miss Berkeley, was in his company and exploring the captain's diary he provided. Silvestre wanted Patricia Fisher, but the attractive blonde would do just as well provided she knew enough.

According to Hugo, Miss Berkeley was the brains leading the research into the San José. The news surprised him, Silvestre acknowledging that he'd dismissed her as too attractive to be clever; a foolish notion if ever there was one.

It wasn't yet time to act, his reason to be at the museum nothing more than a desire to be close to hand when the time came.

It boiled down to whether the blonde woman possessed information he did not. The Aurelia crew found Finn Murphy's body and though Silvestre was able to obtain a copy of the autopsy and recover the treasure they found, he could not know what else they might have uncovered.

Hugo was to watch and assist her and was to do nothing else today no matter who told him he should. The assistant curator had been paid far more than his time was worth, and the fool believed he would live to spend it.

'No loose ends' was a policy Silvestre endorsed at every turn and one which had never let him down. He was close to discovering the final resting place of the San José and its treasure; he could feel it. Fighting his impatience, Silvestre moved through the museum, waiting for the next message from Hugo.

The Man with the Mullet

Captain Danvers walked beside me behind two uniformed officers as they led the way through the building. It had taken forty minutes to get to the Rothman centre which meant it was almost four o'clock by the time we arrived. On the way I'd begun to question if we might not get there to find they had already packed in for the day.

I needn't have worried for they were still performing. The Rothman Centre had multiple studios for filming, six of which were in use today according to the officious-looking woman who insisted we had to log in and would need an escort if we hoped to find where we wanted to go.

Sporting a name badge with 'Terina' on it, she wanted to know the name of the person we were looking for which, of course, I didn't know.

"Well, I cannot very well direct you, if you don't now who you are here to see," Terina replied snippily, happy to have the upper hand.

I tried to describe the man with the mullet which attracted a scoffing sound – she was enjoying being unhelpful.

"Sheila!" I blurted, the name popping into my head. "He was supposed to report to Sheila. Does that help?"

Terina rolled her eyes and sighed. "Stage twelve." Turning to shout for a colleague, she ordered a red-faced young man in his late teens to 'Run us down' to stage twelve and come straight back.

He didn't look like he ever wanted to come back, but he led us through the building, the uniformed cops right on his heels.

"Stage twelve,' he announced, pointing to a pair of doors with a big number twelve across them, one numeral per door. "You have to wait for filming to stop before you can go in." There was a sign hanging on the door that said the same thing: Filming in progress, no entry.

The cops went straight through the doors regardless, pushing them both wide like cowboys entering a wild west saloon.

Someone yelled, "Cut!" in a voice that was quite clearly displeased, and I tracked the sound to find a tubby man in his fifties glaring at my group. "Can't you read?" he stormed.

Captain Danvers chose to respond with, "I can read you your Miranda Rights if you like. This is a police matter, sir. We will be gone in just a few minutes." Twisting his neck to speak to me, he asked, "Do you see him?"

It would have helped if I'd taken one of the photographs from Linda's apartment as a reference, but as it turned out, he was easy to spot. There were only two dozen people in the room and half of them were involved in the production side of things. Half the actors were female, and two of the male actors were bald.

Only one had a mullet.

"Can we get this over with, please, Mrs Fisher?" Captain Danvers pressed. "Do you see the man you suspect?"

The man with the mullet saw when I picked him from the crowd with my eyes and could see the cops in the room. For a man I suspected to have killed someone less than twenty-four hours ago, he looked remarkably calm.

Too calm.

Tendrils of doubt wrapped themselves around my heart.

"There he is!" yelled Gloria, her claim affirmed by similar shouts from Peggy and Pearl. "He's the one I saw in the window! He's the killer!"

The people standing to Mullet Man's left and right stepped away, a space clearing around the killer like he was a magnet with the opposite pole to all those near him.

The calm demeanour was gone, and he was starting to panic. I could see his eyes twitch, looking for a way out and calculating his odds of making it.

The director running the shoot was coming over, angry about the intrusion and about being spoken down to and ignored.

"Who is it you want?" he demanded.

I chose to point. "The man with the mullet."

"Joey? You want Joey?" When the man with the mullet pointed to himself, identifying that he was indeed Joey, the director bellowed, "Joey, get out. We'll film your scene tomorrow if they haven't locked you up."

His remark was intended as a joke and it drew some titters from his people, but Joey looked increasingly worried.

Leaving no opportunity for discussion, the director was heading back to his chair and barking at everyone to take their places before Joey's feet could start to move. In case it wasn't clear, the director added, "Take it outside."

Two minutes later, in the corridor beyond the doors for stage twelve, the uniformed cops were a few yards away where they chatted to kill the time. Joey was pinned up against the wall and surrounded by Captain Danvers, me, the three old ladies who wanted him to be strip searched for weapons, and Jermaine who stood just behind me like a silent guardian.

"Chet's dead?" Joey treated the news like it came as a shock. I know he's an actor, but I didn't think he was faking. "How?"

"He was shot," reported Danvers. "These ladies claim to have seen you attempting to kill him yourself."

"What!" Joey jolted at the suggestion.

"Don't deny it!" snapped Pearl. "We all saw you. You had a length of rope around the poor man's throat, and you were wringing the life out of him."

"Yeah!" added Gloria.

The pedant inside me wanted to point out Joey had been garrotting his victim, not strangling him. It was a technicality though, so I let it pass.

Joey opened his mouth to deny the charge, but stopped, his brain whirring.

"Hold on. Where did you say you saw this?"

Jumping in, I said, "They were on the top deck of a tour bus. You were inside the offices of Houston Investments on the first floor of the Roosevelt Building."

Joey closed his eyes and sagged, but it was relief I could see on his face.

"Yes, you're right, I did have a rope around his neck. We were filming a spy thriller."

My mind jumped to the strange parallel lines I'd found in the carpet.

"Filming. You had cameras mounted on wheels."

Joey's eyes were open, and his look of terror was gone.

"Yes. Wait, if you saw those, why did you think I was trying to kill him?"

The old ladies were looking at each other.

"I didn't see any cameras," said Peggy.

"Nor did I," expressed Gloria.

Pearl pulled a face. "We did only catch a short glimpse," she reminded the other two. "I was looking at the two men. I didn't really notice anything else."

"Mystery solved then," said Captain Danvers to an accompanying huff of air.

"Hardly," I replied. "There's still the small matter that Chet Kowalski was shot and killed last night."

"Yes, thank you for reminding me, Mrs Fisher. Without you I might have forgotten that I have yet another murder to solve." Captain Danvers was not happy with me. "If only I could be out there pursuing the case instead of wasting my time following up nonsense leads with you."

Ignoring him, I asked Joey, "What time did you last see Chet?"

"Oh, when he left the building. Shanice – that's my girlfriend – she works in the building as the receptionist. That's how we knew there was a fully furnished office available for us to use. We don't have much of a budget, as you might imagine. We're trying to shoot a pilot for a TV series so we can sell it to a channel and get the starring roles. Getting a decent acting gig in this town is hard."

"So you don't know the people who worked at Houston Investments?"

"Know them?" Joey looked confused. "I'd never heard of the company until yesterday. Shanice said they shut down like two days ago and told me she could just let us in to use it. I guess I could get her into trouble by telling you that. No one was supposed to know. We were just shooting a short segment of the pilot and needed an office environment. We can't afford film sets."

"Did Chet know the people at Houston Investments?"

Joey thought about it. "I don't think so. He never said anything, and I don't know why he would. It's not exactly our neighbourhood."

His explanation rang true. Shanice had been lying about someone being in the office, but did so to protect her job.

"She told you all to get out, didn't she?" I checked to see if I had that part right.

Joey nodded, his face questioning how I could know that detail.

"Yeah, I got a call from her to say there were three mad old ..." his words trailed off as he realised he was talking about the three women currently looking at him, their expressions imploring him to finish his sentence. "... dears," he concluded weakly, "making a fuss. Said they'd seen a..." I saw the cogs in his head align, "murder. Now I get it. Shanice said she'd been forced to call the cops and we needed to make ourselves scarce. We were about finished anyway. I think Chet said he had a shift at work and was going there when I last saw him. That would have been just after one, I guess."

I was no closer to figuring out who killed Chet Kowalski and still didn't have the faintest idea what happened at Houston Investments. Worse yet, I'd made Captain Danvers' job harder, not easier. Maybe it was time to let it go.

I could accept that it was the right thing to do, but there were a few matters to tie up first.

Speaking to Joey, I asked, "Have you heard from Shanice in the last few hours?"

"She'll be at work, and she knows not to disturb me when I'm on set. Like I said, getting a break in this town is hard, so when you get a role, even when it's a tiny one that barely pays enough to make it worth turning up, you have to suck it up and make friends with the right people. Having your phone ring during filming would get me tossed out and never invited back. Why are you asking?"

"Because she wasn't at work, and it looked like she left in a hurry. Also," I didn't think I was going to have to break this piece of news – I'd come here expecting to catch a killer, "someone broke into your apartment and trashed it. I think they were looking for something."

Joey whipped his phone out the moment I made him worry about his girlfriend. It was switched off and was taking its sweet time coming back to life.

136

"Looking for something? What could they be looking for? We haven't got anything worth stealing."

The screen on his phone lit up and it played a little tinkle of music. He had it to his ear a heartbeat later, a call placed to Shanice. Not that she answered.

He was starting to look worried and even Captain Danvers was taking an interest.

"She's not answering," Joey stated the obvious. "I have to go look for her." He was already starting to walk away, his mind on a new problem.

"Where, Joey?" I asked, getting in his way, but not actually impeding his departure. It was more the soft tone of my voice that halted his feet. "Where will you look for her?"

"I – I ... I don't know," he conceded, his shoulders sagging.

I could imagine his desire to do something was almost impossible to resist, but I stopped him because I still had questions and I was willing to bet he knew more about the situation than he realised.

"Joey, did Shanice ever say anything about the firms at her building? Did she ever mention Houston Investments?"

Joey shook his head. "I already told you, I never heard of them before two days ago when Shanice said she had an abandoned office where we could shoot a scene for the pilot."

A little itch at the back of skull changed what I was going to ask next.

"Did Shanice know Chet?"

He shrugged. "Sure. He came by the apartment a few times. I think she was with us in a bar once or twice. I've known Chet for years, ever since we both didn't get the same part and chose to go for a beer to drown our sorrows."

"How were you funding the movie?" I hadn't thought about it before, but Chet worked in a coffee shop – an honourable profession, but not a highly paid one, and Joey had already complained about how little his tiny acting role today was paying. They both lived with their girlfriends in apartments that were sparsely furnished and probably cheap to rent.

Captain Danvers lost his patience before Joey could answer.

"Mrs Fisher," he grumbled angrily, "you have strung this out for long enough. There is nothing here. Your friends did not witness a murder as we established yesterday, and the unfortunate fact that Chet Kowalski was subsequently murdered the same day has nothing to do with any of this. I am going to escort you back to your ship and you will stay there. Is that understood? I am revoking your New York privileges. If you step back on shore, I will arrest you for wasting police time and interfering in an ongoing investigation."

Frustrated, yet aware I had done nothing but try the man's patience and make his job harder, I pushed for Joey to answer.

"He borrowed money from a loan shark, didn't he?"

Captain Danvers opened his mouth to say something, but I was able to get in first.

"Please, Captain. When we went to Chet's apartment, his girlfriend was there with two burly men. They were intimidating her, and they wanted money. Ten thousand dollars that Chet borrowed and failed to repay." I shifted my gaze to Joey once more. "That's how he was paying for the pilot, wasn't it."

Joey looked awful, but not in the sense that he was guilty of knowing the truth.

"Oh, man," he sighed. "He told me his uncle died and left him some cash. I knew he was lying; you can just tell sometimes, right? I should have challenged it. Is that what got him killed?"

I looked at Captain Danvers to see what he thought of the latest development. My brain was working fast, trying to piece things together. That Chet might have met his end at the hands of the loan sharks was a new consideration. Until a few minutes ago, I was still looking for the man Gloria's Gang saw strangling him.

Danvers let a tired laugh out and reached up with one hand to rub his forehead. When he met my eyes again, the amusement was gone.

"Mrs Fisher, loan sharks do not kill the people who owe them money, they break their fingers, or threaten to hurt their loved ones. How can a dead person repay the debt?"

I swore inside my head. That was so obvious. But Chet *had* borrowed the money.

The police captain lifted his left arm to form a barrier and used the right to indicate that I should start moving in the other direction.

"Move, Mrs Fisher. I can deliver you back to the ship in cuffs if you prefer."

He wasn't kidding.

"Does that mean I can go?" asked Joey. "I need to try to find Shanice."

Over his shoulder, Danvers said, "Sure. Good luck, kid."

Gloria said, "Wait, what's happening? What about Houston Investments and all their missing staff? What about that South American bunch of lowlifes who want their money back and think we must know where it is?"

Captain Danvers' face scrunched up, his whole body cringing. "South American bunch?"

Pop Star Lookalike

"Mrs Fisher, that is about the craziest thing I have heard yet." Captain Danvers' face was a mask of disbelief, but he hadn't stopped listening. "You want me to believe you just survived an encounter with the Columbian Cartel?"

I gave him a kind of half shrug.

"That's what you just said," he argued.

"No, I said they looked and sounded like they were from a South American nation. There's quite a few of those to pick from."

Danvers gritted his teeth, frustrated, but clearly also kind of excited at the possibility of a lead into a case he needed to solve. With his eyes closed, he pressed me to answer a simple question.

"I know you gave a statement when the cops arrived, but just for my own sanity, what did their leader look like? Can you describe him?"

"Oh, um, ok." I was going to start with the man's height and hair colour, my eyes rolling up and left to engage the memory portion of my brain.

Jermaine said, "He looks like Enrique Iglesias from fifteen years ago at the height of his career."

The police captain's weary eyes snapped open.

"That's right!" I exclaimed. When I first saw him, I knew there was something familiar about his face. I might never have connected the dots, but now that Jermaine had said it …"

Danvers shook his head at me. "That's Manolo Ravassa. He's the son of the boss. THE boss of the Columbian Cartel. There are rumours that he'd been seen here, but the man is like a ghost." I got more head shaking. "You wander into town, decide to solve a murder even though the ladies in question didn't witness anything of the sort, only to then find yourself embroiled in … what? A money laundering conspiracy involving one of the largest and oldest organised crime families ever to operate on American soil? How do you do that?"

I wasn't sure what the right response might be, so I went with, "It's a skill?"

He repeated my words, a sad chuckle slipping out.

"Okay, oh mighty skilled one. You have my attention. Tell me more about Houston Investments."

"Well, I don't exactly know anything," I started, "but, the staff working there left so suddenly, they didn't stop to take their personal belongings with them and now my team cannot find them. That was two days ago. Not one former employee at Houston Investments is at home and none of them are answering their phones. So far, my team managed to track down one person who is staying with his sister in Buffalo."

"Buffalo?" Danvers repeated, his face betraying his confusion. "Why would anyone ever go to Buffalo?"

I had no opinion on the location and would struggle to find it on a map.

"I thought Chet Kowalski's murder and whatever happened at Houston Investments had to be connected. I've been following a trail of clues and attempting to join the dots since yesterday afternoon."

Shaking his head as if to clear it, Danvers said, "And now you think the two things might not be connected. Is that it?"

I was still piecing things together inside my head, encouraging my brain to work the problem as fast as it could. Chet and Joey were in the Houston Investment firm's offices purely out of coincidence and the ladies didn't actually see Chet being killed. What they saw was a hopeful actor trying to make a success of himself.

Captain Danvers waited for my response, so I said, "I don't know."

He chuckled in a sad, defeated way and threw his arms in the air.

"Of course you don't."

"But look at what we do know," I implored. "Something triggers the entire staff to flee the area taking their families with them. Chet goes there two days later and is killed the same day. I went there yesterday and had a sniper shooting at me today. An hour ago I had what you now assure me were members of the Columbian Cartel asking me questions about Houston Investments and demanding their money back. There is an obvious conclusion here."

Danvers said it for me. "Houston Investments were money laundering for the cartel and lost the money. Someone got inside and ripped them off. The staff left town because they knew what would happen to them if they stayed and the Columbians have been chasing anyone who might know anything ever since."

"They've got Shanice then," Gloria concluded. "That's why she's missing from work and why her place had been searched."

Danvers focused on what he wanted to know. "You have people trying to find the staff of this investment firm right now?"

"I do."

Right on cue, my phone rang, and I punched a mental fist into the air when I saw Schneider's name on the screen.

Winking at Captain Danvers, I said, "This is them right now." With my right index finger I tapped the green button to connect the call and then the speaker icon so everyone would be able to hear. "Schneider, I have you on speaker. I'm with the local police. Did you succeed in talking to Benny Crozier?"

"Not exactly," Schneider replied.

Danvers hiked an eyebrow at the cryptic response, but didn't say anything.

Schneider knew his remark needed to be qualified, so he kept talking.

"His sister phoned back just a couple of minutes ago. Benny came home, but when she told him we had called, he grabbed his bags, got into his car, and drove off at speed. She said he tried to convince her to go with him. He wouldn't say what was going on or why he was scared, and when she refused to go, he left without her."

I gave Captain Danvers a meaningful look; he was invested and fervently wanted me to be able to give him information he could use.

"That's not what you called to tell me though," I guessed, expecting there to be more.

"No, there's more. Benny ran out so fast he left his phone behind, so his sister accessed his list of contacts and used her own phone to call Benny's boss."

"William Chalice?" I hazarded, remembering the name of the firm's CEO.

Schneider said, "Yeah, that's right. Anyway, he didn't answer his phone and I think that's where we got lucky."

Confused, I said, "I don't follow. How does that help us?"

"Because his mother answered." I could hear the satisfaction in Schneider's voice. "She lives in Park Slope, Brooklyn and has her son staying with her. I told her we were old friends, that I was in New York for the night, and hoped to catch up with him. She gave me her address so I could surprise him and promised not to tell her son about my call."

I couldn't fight the big grin spreading across my face – my friends really are amazing.

143

Captain Danvers said, "Park Slope? We can be there in twenty minutes."

Schneider agreed to meet us there.

Captain Danvers could have sent a unit to pick up William Chalice, but going in person was the right thing to do. The police captain looked as battered and broken as ever, but the chance to get some answers and maybe close one of his open cases – Chet Kowalski's murder, was too tempting to leave to anyone else. Add in the tantalising possibility that he might find out something useful about the Columbian Cartel, who were moving in to take over the New York criminal enterprises, and there was no way he could leave it to one of his subordinates.

Sitting in the passenger seat of his car, I silently ran through what I knew and tried, yet again, to correlate the clues.

I didn't get very far.

The missing money was key to it all. Or so I allowed myself to believe. Looking from the outside, it appeared to be the catalyst for everything that came after. A hacker gets inside Houston Investment's money – I had no idea how, but they did. That the money belonged to the cartel explained why nothing got reported. The *Wall Street Journal* heard rumours and the firm's entire staff were missing so their journalists were unable to confirm any facts.

Chet was killed, but was that because someone saw him in the building and assumed he knew something about the missing money? Maybe, but was it the cartel who killed him or the cybercriminal trying to cover their tracks?

Also, why only kill Chet? Joey said nothing about being targeted – my brain was only now looking at that angle. Joey said they had camera guys there too, so why were none of them put in the crosshairs?

Unable to unpick things, I closed my eyes and prayed William Chalice would have some answers.

William Chalice

I had no idea Brooklyn was so pretty. Envisaging concrete and red brick as far as the eyes could see, I was shocked to find avenues filled with trees and tidy front yards resplendent with evergreen colour. Away from the bustle of Manhattan, the suburb boasted bird song and the sound of kids playing. It was a place I could imagine living.

Jermaine came around to open my door before jogging back to the taxi parked behind Captain Danvers car. There he helped Gloria's Gang out of the cab and onto their scooters. They all had fold up models that fit easily between the boots of the two cars.

"Coo, this is nice," said Gloria, looking around.

Schneider and pals were on their way, but Captain Danvers was not of a mind to wait. Boldly, he used the iron knocker and then the doorbell to attract the attention of someone inside the house.

It was just one in a long line of what would be called terrace houses back home in England. The front doors were all set a yard off the ground up a short flight of stone steps. The buildings looked to be a hundred years old, but the ironwork fencing running along the edge of the postage-stamp sized yards and up the side of the steps was in fine condition, the jet-black paint still shiny.

145

Danvers didn't give the residents more than few seconds to get to the door before hammering again. Not that he made it sound like he was trying to break down the door, and he didn't call out that it was the police, which I thought he would.

I surmised that he stayed silent so as not to scare the person inside into running. He'd parked down the street too, and I suspected now this was part of the same strategy - a person might look out and see the police car outside their house otherwise.

Just when he raised his fist to rap a third time, I heard the sound of the lock operating and the door opened to reveal a woman in her late sixties. She wore jeans and house slippers below an orange woollen top with a designer logo embroidered over her left breast.

"Hello." She spoke with a Brooklyn accent. "Are you the man I spoke with on the phone? William's friend?"

Captain Danvers held up his badge.

"No, mam." He introduced himself. "I need to speak with William. Can you fetch him, please?"

"Oh, you'll have to come in. He's been refusing to answer the door ever since he arrived. Is he in some kind of trouble?" she asked, backing away to let Captain Danvers in and peering around him to take in the entourage following him up the steps.

Gloria, Peggy, and Pearl were off their scooters and complaining about the stairs they now needed to climb. They were all capable enough though, their mode of transport there to make getting around easier, not because it would otherwise be impossible.

"He's ever such a good boy, you know," William's mum continued.

Drawing level with her, I extended my hand.

"Hello, I'm Patricia," I chose to leave out my last name and hope she didn't recognise me; it would just be a distraction.

146

She gripped my offered hand for just a brief second. "Sally." Captain Danvers was ahead and walking down the hall to access the rest of the house. Sally hurried along to lead him, probably so he wouldn't be able to explore her home at will.

"William," she called out. "William there are some people here to see you."

We all heard his expletive.

"It's the police," Sally added.

There was a long pause before we heard the voice upstairs say, "The police?"

Captain Danvers got in before Sally could answer.

"Yes, Mr Chalice. We have a few questions for you about Houston Investments. Can you come down, please?"

He got no reply.

Jermaine looked at me, his eyes meeting mine to confirm I too had heard the sound of a window opening.

Captain Danvers sighed. "I hate it when they run."

Knowing he was the fittest and fastest by a long way, Jermaine was already moving.

"I'll cover the front," Danvers called out, but I was certain William had chosen to go out the back.

Shocked at the turn of events, Sally looked pale.

"What's happening?" she wanted to know, following me as I took off after Jermaine. "How much trouble is William in? Is this something to do with why he hasn't been going to work?"

By the time I found the back door, Jermaine had hold of William, a man I recognised from his photograph on the firm's website. Jermaine wasn't restraining him as he might another person – so far as I could work out, William had done nothing wrong. Instead, Jermaine had one hand on William's shoulder to guide him back toward the house.

"It really is the police?" William asked, sounding like he was surprised to still be alive. Gloria, Peggy, and Pearl were hanging out the back door, the sight of three old ladies enough to make William doubt it was a hit squad.

I asked a question I dearly wanted answered, "Who were you expecting?"

William's mouth stayed shut as he steadfastly refused to say, but Sally wanted to know too.

"William, just what have you got yourself mixed up in?" she demanded, her tone that of a mother admonishing a little boy. "What is it that you're not telling me?"

Inside the house, with Jermaine once again making tea for everyone, I finally got some answers.

"I knew it was dirty money, but what was I supposed to do?" he lamented.

"Tell them no," snapped William's mother as though it were obvious.

"I would have been dead five minutes later, mom."

Sally looked set to argue, but Captain Danvers said, "Let him speak, please." To William, he prompted, "Whose money was it?" He already suspected the answer, but needed to hear William say it.

William huffed out a breath. "The Columbian Cartel."

Captain Danvers' features filled with hope.

In contrast, Sally reacted as though she'd been slapped. "You work for the mob! You bought me this house! Is this bought with drug money?" She sounded and looked horrified. I probably would be too.

"No, mom! This is a recent thing. I bought this house five years ago and I don't work for anyone. I'm my own boss."

The Columbian Cartel. That *was* who I met in the street earlier, just after the sniper showed up. They were after their money and wanted to know what I had done with it or what I knew.

"They approached you?" I checked.

William nodded. "An accountant did. I didn't know it was crime money at the time. It looked like a legitimate investment."

Danvers' eyes lit up. "An accountant? You met their accountant?"

Peggy asked, "Why is that exciting? I worked for the IRS for almost sixty years and never once met an accountant who wasn't as dry and boring as dust."

I knew the answer. "It's how the cops beat them. Get to the money of an organised crime enterprise and you can find out everything. People will lie. They will go to jail rather than speak out against an organisation, so putting people like the Columbian Cartel behind bars is almost impossible."

"Unless you have hard evidence," agreed Captain Danvers. "They hide the movement of money so we cannot catch them in the act of having it, let alone prove where it came from, but there is always an accountant. Get to them and we just might get everything." Talking to himself, he said, "Catch these guys and I might actually manage to get the chief off my back."

William spoke up. "Sorry. I said the accountant contacted me. I never actually met him. When the meeting happened, it was with three youngish men. I didn't have any reason to believe it wasn't legitimate at the time. I only found out where it was coming from when I went through the legal process of financial acquisition checks. The men all spoke with a heavy accent which made me ask if the money was coming in from outside the US. The moment I raised the subject of the money's origin - the process exists to stop us laundering huge amounts of cash for criminals - they put a gun in my face. I invested their money, or I died, and they would move on to the next firm. I tried to back out ... tried to say it wouldn't be possible for the firm to handle their money, but there was a dead rat under my pillow the next morning."

Peggy pulled a face.

Captain Danvers interrupted.

"But organised crime families don't invest money. There's too much chance it will be identified and seized."

William shrugged. "I know, but they weren't asking for financial advice. They were getting that from their own accountant. The boss ... don't ask me his name because they were very good at not giving me any, he believed he was going to make money by investing what he had. I mean, he wasn't wrong. Give me a few million dollars to play around with and I can make a fortune."

William was boasting about his wizardry with finances until he caught the expressions on our faces.

I spoke his name to get William looking my way.

"What happened with the money? It went missing, didn't it?"

William nodded sombrely, his face aimed at the carpet until he started speaking. With a glum expression, he met my eyes and tried to explain.

"No one else at the firm had any idea where the money came from. I listed it under the name 'H.G. Knowles' to make it look like any other investor. I didn't know what else I could do, and it was supposed to be a temporary investment. I think their accountant told them they could make money on the side; that's certainly the impression they had, and they were not taking no for an answer. I knew if I complied they would just keep coming back and they would own me, but they warned me what would happen if I went to the cops."

Danvers cut in. "William, the men you met with, how do you know it was the Columbian Cartel?"

William didn't have to think about his answer. "They all but told me. Plus, you know, they were Columbian, their money clearly came from a shady source, and they were happy to cut my feet off and make me eat them if I didn't do as they said."

While I reeled from that particular mental image, Captain Danvers asked one more question.

"Can you describe the men you spoke with?"

William's nerves were frayed, that much was clear to anyone with eyes. I doubted he'd slept in days, and the act of talking to us about it was making him feel sick. It was also his only way out and I think he knew it.

With a sigh, he looked Captain Danvers straight in the eye.

"The one in charge looked just like Enrique Iglesias used to. Tan skin, dark brown eyes, unfairly handsome." William was tubby with pale skin and a pudgy face that a mother would love, but other women might struggle to find attractive.

If there had been any doubt in my mind before, it was gone now. The big boss of the Columbian Cartel dispatched his son to New York so he could run the business. Now the son was scrambling to fix a problem of his own making and probably trying to do so before his father found out.

Chasing after however much ...

"William, how much money are we talking about?" It surprised me that none of us had thought to ask that question yet.

With a lopsided apology on his face, William said, "Forty million."

Gloria whistled, a low sound of appreciation. "That would buy a lot of donuts."

"Cashflow," I murmured.

Everyone looked my way.

"Yesterday, in the mattress shop, the ladies said the men were arguing about payment.

"That's right," said Pearl. "The Columbians were arguing about money. It sounded like they were temporarily short."

Lose forty million dollars and the boss's son ... I had to dredge my memory for his name – Manolo Ravassa – was probably doing everything he could to keep hold of the money he still had.

Trying not to think too hard about the fact that Gloria, Peggy, and Pearl shot a whole bunch of the cartel members, I pushed William to explain how the money went missing.

All he could do was shrug. "Someone got inside our system and transferred all their money out. It was gone, and I knew there was no way I could tell them without ending up at the bottom of the Hudson River."

"So you told the staff at your firm what had happened and warned them to get out."

William nodded. "I did. I couldn't report it because it was crime money, and I couldn't get it back. Honestly, I'm glad you found me; waiting to get caught by them has been making me sick."

Captain Danvers pushed off the arms of his chair to rise to his feet.

"Mr Chalice, you need to come downtown with me. I need to contact some people in the serious crimes division and probably the FBI. You are going to have to testify to everything you've just told me. That's for later. First, I need to get you somewhere safe."

The cab that brought Gloria's Gang left the moment they got out, but we would be able to find another. Captain Danvers was heading back to his precinct, but we were not invited, and there was no reason for us to be involved.

Of course, there was still the small matter of Chet's murder, though my assumption now was that the Cartel killed him. They must have been watching the Roosevelt Building and saw him in the Houston Investment offices. They would have seen Joey and the camera guys too, but it was Chet they chose to interrogate.

They would have learned the truth from him and in so doing discovered there was no reason to pursue Joey or the others. They killed Chet to cover their tracks and then put the sniper on me when they saw me in the same office a day later.

Hold on though. If they sent the sniper, why did they turn up to ask me questions two minutes after the shooting stopped? If they wanted to quiz me about my involvement – which made sense now – then shooting me first made no sense.

I was still trying to figure that out when they arrived.

Trapped

We were just leaving Sally's house. Captain Danvers was down at street level with William who was waiting for his mother. Whether he wanted her in attendance or not never got discussed; she was going with him and that was that.

I was just stepping down the last step, Gloria using my shoulder as an additional support while Jermaine hung back to make sure the twins were okay.

Too lost in thought to notice the procession of cars coming our way at speed, it was only when Jermaine grabbed me that I looked around to spot the danger.

Not that it made any difference; there was nowhere we could go.

On the peaceful street, the late autumn sun created dappled shadows where it passed through the tree branches. Parked cars lined both sides of the street to leave enough room for two cars to pass in opposite directions in the middle.

The cartel, arriving in the same cars we saw them in last time, filled the middle of the road to make passing them impossible. The doors opened before the lead car came to a stop twenty yards past our position and men with guns hit the street with fierce expressions aimed our way.

We had no car into which we could easily escape, and any thoughts of running were eroded by the presence of Gloria's Gang who were yet to remount their scooters. The cavalcade of cars cut off the street in both directions before Captain Danvers had time to react.

There was a gun on him before he could get to his radio.

"I wouldn't," advised the man pointing a gun at the police captain's chest. More than thirty members of the Columbian Cartel joined him within a few seconds.

News headlines when I took down the Godmother and the Alliance of Families claimed it was 'The end of organised crime', or some such sensational nonsense that helped them sell copies.

It wasn't anything of the sort. Thousands of criminals were arrested in the wake of exposing the combined crime families, but there were some, like the Columbian's, who chose to not be part of the Godmother's alliance. With most of their competition removed, they were able to flourish. Smaller organisations popped into existence to help fill the void, so organised crime merely grew a new face.

Like a hydra, I helped to cut off one head and two more grew in its place.

William squealed in fright and bolted for the house.

"Quick, Mom! Get back inside!" he yelled.

The sound of several dozen guns being cocked caused his feet to falter.

The men came forward, some holding their guns on my group while others used their hands to pat us down.

"Here! You watch what you're fondling," snapped Peggy.

"Yeah!" echoed Gloria. Followed by her whispering, "Do you want my number?" to the young man patting her down.

They were a little handsy, I noted, but pushed the unnecessary cupping from my mind. I was shocked they hadn't just shot us given how our previous encounter ended.

"This one is a cop, boss," reported the man disarming Captain Danvers.

"That's right!" snarled Pearl. "He's a captain. You lot best clear off before he arrests you all."

Danvers twitched his eyes in my direction. Our situation was precarious to say the least and the old ladies were not helping.

In response to Pearl's outburst, the Columbian Cartel guys exchanged looks and sniggered. A few acted scared, biting their fingernails or shivering, much to the amusement of their fellow gunmen.

"Mr Chalice," called a voice. I turned my head to see Manolo Ravassa exiting the backseat of one of the cars. "Mr Chalice you should have run a lot further and a lot faster. Taking my money was a mistake."

I blinked a couple of times. "Wait. You think he's got your money?"

Manolo was on the street now and coming my way.

"Got it. Knows where it is. Whichever. He's going to get it back and then he's going to die in a most unpleasant manner."

Sally shrieked in horror and William whimpered.

"I don't have it," he wailed. "I never did. Someone hacked into our computers and transferred it all out. Killing me won't get it back. I can help you though. Give me time and I'll make it all back with fresh investments. I'll even use my own money."

"Enough." Manolo was bright enough to not want to execute anyone in the street. Like earlier, he planned to take us somewhere else. "Pack them into the cars. All of them."

"What for?" demanded Gloria. "We haven't got your money?"

Manolo shot her a 'really?' look. "You shot twelve of my men. They would like to return the favour."

Gloria said, "Oh, yeah. I'd forgotten about that." Dropping her voice to a whisper, she hissed at me, "Those bazookas don't sound like such a bad idea now, do they?"

Actually, they sounded like a terrible idea, but I didn't say that. Instead, I asked a question.

"Why did you kill Chet Kowalski?"

Manolo Ravassa shot me a look.

"Not that I am stupid enough to admit a crime in front of a cop, even one who will be dead shortly, I have no idea who Chet Kowalski is."

Danvers spoke for the first time.

"If you kill me, every cop in New York will come gunning for you."

Manolo shrugged his indifference.

"I'll take that risk."

Now here's a thing about the way my brain works. I solve what appear to be complex and confusing mysteries that no one else can unravel, but I don't really know how I do it. I poke about and ask questions. I examine the clues and try to join the dots, but usually the answer just pops into my head at some point along the way.

And that's precisely what happened. Standing on the sidewalk outside Sally's house, with my hands at shoulder height and thirty armed Columbians planning to kidnap and kill me and everyone I was with, I suddenly figured it out.

"Which one of you is the accountant?" I asked.

"No stalling," insisted Manolo, encouraging his men to get us moving with a whistle and a jerk of his head.

"If you want your money back, you'd better listen to me." I was playing a risky game and I really was stalling for time, but if there was chance we could get out of this alive, this was it. "I think I can get you every cent of it, but not if you hurt me or my friends."

Manolo sneered, "You will tell me everything and more when we start cutting pieces off you. Mr Chalice will tell me where the money is and beg for me to end his life by the time I am through."

The mental images his words conjured were enough to make me feel sick and I had to take a breath before I pushed on.

"He's telling the truth. He doesn't have it. Do you really think a man with forty million at his disposal would be hiding in his mother's house? No one is looking for him ..."

"We are," argued Manolo. "I have men at every airport in the city."

"Nevertheless, if he had forty million dollars of your money, don't you think he would have found a way to escape?"

I saw a flicker of doubt cross the Columbian mob boss's face.

"Your accountant took it," I stated boldly, filling my voice with confidence so he would believe I somehow knew that to be true. The skin around his eyes tightened slightly and I spotted him glance toward the cars.

Was the accountant in one of them?

"Your accountant suggested putting the money into a hedge fund, didn't he?"

Manolo looked at me again, but said nothing.

"Boss, we need to get off the street," urged the same lieutenant who hadn't wanted to hang around when they cornered us in the alley earlier. This time Manolo listened.

However, just when I thought we were all going to be shoved into car boots to be questioned somewhere else, something unexpected occurred.

"She's right," rang out a voice from further down the street.

I think everyone turned to see who had spoken. A man was walking past the cars idling in the middle of the road, a little girl with blonde hair in a ponytail holding his hand. It was a bizarre sight that stood in counterpoint to the armed men filling the street.

They allowed him to pass, the new arrival heading directly for the boss just a few yards in front of me.

Manolo shifted his body to face the man as he approached.

"I hope you will forgive the intrusion," he said, his voice raised slightly so he would he heard.

"Boss we really need to move," urged the nervous lieutenant. "This isn't safe."

Ignoring his concerns, Manolo offered his hand for the newcomer to shake.

"What are you doing here, Alan?" he asked when their hands met. "You know something about this matter?"

"I was offered a contract earlier today." To my surprise, the man nodded his head in my direction. "For her."

A contract? What did that mean?

The Columbian boss jinked an eyebrow. "You missed?"

Alan let a smile tease one side of his mouth. "Not exactly. I saw you speaking to her and that raised a few questions. I did a little digging, asked a few questions ..."

"Daddy?" the little girl interrupted.

"Not now, sweetie," Alan crouched a little to bring his head closer to the little girl's height. "Daddy needs to do a little bit of business. Then we'll go for ice cream, okay?"

"Kay."

"Sorry," Alan apologised for his daughter. "Now, where was I?"

"Boss!" griped the lieutenant.

Manolo held up an index finger, making it quite clear he wasn't ready to be disturbed. "You were confirming my accountant is behind my missing forty million."

159

"Oh, yes. That's right."

Manolo turned his head to the side, looking to the cars when he shouted, "Jakob!"

One of the gunmen standing near the cars gripped a back door and opened it. A head ventured out, the face attached to it bearing an uncertain expression.

"Hey!" yelled William, "That's the IT guy who came to fix a glitch on our server last week!"

"No, I'm not," insisted the man in the car. He said the words, but I'm not sure anyone believed them.

Alan spoke to the boss. "He hired me to carry out the hit on her." He dipped his head in my direction again. "I assumed the hit was assigned by you until you showed up and started to talk to her. Speaking to a few people about town, I am given to understand you have an unexpected cashflow issue."

Manolo's lips twitched. "Indeed," he replied, his eyes squinting at the person being encouraged to leave the confines of the car in which he still hid.

Sally asked, "All cleared up then? Your guy did it, not my son? We'll just be going then, okay?" She pulled her keys out, intending to get back inside her house, but that was never going to be an option.

Manolo Ravassa said, "I'm afraid not. Take them. Dispose of them." He delivered the death sentence with the calm demeanour of a man ordering pizza and the men who'd been hovering just a few yards away awaiting final instructions came for us.

Thankfully, I have friends.

Enraged Steel Rhinoceros

I don't think anyone other than me and possibly Jermaine saw Schneider arrive at the end of the street just after the cartel filled it. He was with Sam, Molly, and Pippin, the four of them assessing what they could see and then acting accordingly.

They would call the police, of that I felt certain, but the cops were not going to arrive in time or in sufficient numbers to help us, so when they vanished back out of sight around the corner, I fervently hoped they were cooking up a plan B.

If we were on the ship, they would be armed, but ashore they were essentially civilians with no more power or authority than a postman. Not that a shootout would save us. Not twice in one day.

Thankfully, they chose to go with something less subtle.

I heard the yelling before I saw the truck.

Barrelling around the corner and into the street, a blue and white cement mixer came so fast I thought the wheels on one side were going to leave the tarmac. The roaring engine could not be missed, but just in case, the driver honked the truck's airhorn. Like an enraged steel rhinoceros, it charged at the line of cars filling the middle of the street.

It was hard to see between the trees and cars, but as it came closer, I realised it wasn't Schneider driving as my brain assumed it would be, but Molly, my former housemaid, the diminutive woman barely tall enough to see over the steering wheel.

The shouting came from the construction workers who were giving chase. Just ahead of them, Sam, Pippin, and Schneider did their best to use the cement mixer as a shield from the bullets which began to fly their way when the Columbian Cartel recognised what was about to happen.

The man with the little girl yanked her into his arms and ran, tearing down the street and away from the danger.

Jermaine grabbed Sally and William, yanking them off the steps and down to the street as the lead began to fly. He didn't stay there though.

Yelling that I should take cover, Jermaine leapt over my ducking head to land vicious blows with his windmilling feet. Distracted by the insane cement truck coming their way, the Columbian thugs didn't see him coming.

Jermaine took out five of them before I could even get my body to the ground. Danvers proved to be no slouch either. While I chose to throw myself out of harm's way, he swung a right cross at the nearest thug, disarmed him, and started firing.

Jermaine's efforts resulted in more weapons landing with a clatter on the hard surface of the street, but Gloria's whoop of joy at being able to arm herself again was drowned out by the terrible rending sound of metal ploughing through metal.

The cement mixer went through the first car like a freight train hitting a cardboard box. The crumpled remains became a hood ornament for the next one in line and the giant truck, gloopy cement dripping from its rear end, kept going like the obstacles in its path were insignificant.

Gunfire echoed all around me; a veritable wall of noise.

Of the thirty or so thugs who turned up with their boss, at least half were down, and I had a firing squad assembled to my left where Gloria, Peggy, and Pearl were emptying the weapons they'd recovered from the unconscious bodies Jermaine left behind. To my right, Captain Danvers had his radio back and was doing much the same thing while barking orders at whoever was there to receive them.

Risking a look, I raised my head to see past the parked cars I hunkered behind for safety. The Columbians were in full retreat.

Again.

If street cred gets you respect among criminal gangs, these guys were going to be the laughingstock of the city. Twice in one day they'd been routed by a trio of old ladies on mobility scooters.

Gingerly, I got to my feet. Sirens were heading our way, this time being led to the right spot by their own police captain.

The cement truck had finally come to a halt. After battering its way through six cars, the resulting mess finally created enough of a plug between the parked cars on either side to stop it.

Molly dared to peek out from her hiding place down below the steering wheel. The shooting had stopped, and she could see running figures heading for the end of the block where they could turn left or right and get out of sight.

Before they could get there, police cars, their lights and sirens in full effect, screeched to a halt to block off the Columbians' escape. Like something from a movie, the cartel suddenly had forty guns aimed their way, the cops hunkered behind their vehicles for protection.

"Are you okay, Mrs Fisher?" asked Sam, arriving at my side rather breathlessly.

I was back on my feet, my limbs operational though my brain was voting for strike action until the citizens of the world agreed to stop trying to kill me.

"Mrs Fisher?" Sam tried again, his goofy grin absent for once. He was concerned for me, the worry in his eyes enough to jolt me out of my dreamlike state.

I placed a hand on his arm. "I'm fine, Sam, thank you. You should check on your grandmother."

Sam sniggered. "Granny? Granny is fine, Mrs Fisher. She's bragging about shooting someone in the bum."

And so she was. My ears were ringing from all the shooting, but when I chose to listen, I could hear the three old ladies comparing their shooting skills and arguing over who was the best shot.

Feeling really rather weary, I checked behind and reversed to the steps of Sally's house where I sat myself on the cool concrete. My beautiful coat was most likely already ruined; too much rolling around on the ground had ensued and I still had blood on it from the sniper attack, but so far as I could see everyone I cared about was still alive and in one piece.

That was a miracle in itself.

Sam left me to check on his grandmother anyway, the three old dears fussing around him as they always do.

Schneider and Pippin were trying to wrench the cement truck's door open and having no luck – there was just too much twisted steel going on. Molly opened the window on the passenger side, sliding out that way to be caught by the guys.

The construction workers who were giving chase when I first saw them, had the good sense to fall back when the shooting started. They were coming forward again now, that male bravado thing making them all come though they were doing so cautiously. I think they could see the cement truck was trashed, but that the 'thieves' took it for good reason.

More cops were arriving behind them, pulling into the blocked street to deploy from their vehicles and I could hear Captain Danvers coordinating it all. His voice carried over the hubbub of noise, booming commands shouted rather than sent over the airwaves.

Watching him, I saw him put his fingers in his mouth to emit a shrill whistle. Catching the attention of half the cops in the street, he aimed a hand at one in particular, the young cop running to receive his instruction before darting away again to perform a task.

Catching me in the act of observing his work, Danvers narrowed his eyes at me and shook his head. I think the message was supposed to be 'This is all your fault', so I waved and smiled like we were old friends. His hand moved and I think he was going to make a rude gesture when he changed his mind and started to walk toward me.

A cop stopped him, wanting to ask a question. Danvers said something I couldn't hear, gave the cop a slap on the shoulder, and sent him on his way. They were dealing with the situation as professionals in full view of hundreds of New York residents who were out of their homes and watching from the steps of their houses, or filling in the gaps at either end of the street where hastily erected barriers were keeping them back.

Paramedics were beginning to arrive which was a good thing because there were a whole bunch of injured people.

Jermaine returned to my side, arriving just before Captain Danvers.

"Are you hurt, madam?"

I shook my head. "No, sweetie. I'm just fine. At least, it's nothing a gin and tonic won't fix." I meant it too. It had been a crazy twenty-four hours, but it was done. The mystery of Houston Investments was solved and the people who worked there could return home now, safe in the knowledge that the cartel, whose money they were accused of stealing, were heading to jail.

Danvers lowered his backside onto the step so he was sitting next to me and we were both looking out at the street.

"Mrs Fisher ..." he began.

"Patricia," I cut in. "I think we can go with first names at this point."

A wry grin curled the corners of his mouth.

"Danny," he replied.

I cocked an eyebrow. "Danny Danvers?"

He laughed a little.

"Patricia, are you planning to stay in New York?"

"Stay? No, I'll be leaving as soon as the ship sails. Why do you ask?" I knew why, but wanted to hear him say it.

He chose instead to ask another question.

"Do you plan to ever return?"

It was my turn to let a smile caress my face.

"Actually, I was thinking I might ask my benefactor to let me stay in his penthouse suite ..."

"Over my dead body!" snapped Danny, shooting his head around to see if I was being serious.

In truth I had no idea if the Maharaja owned a place in New York, but it seemed a fairly safe bet that he would.

Danny looked about ready to have a heart attack, so while I wanted to string him along a bit further, I chose to let him off the hook.

"My dear Captain Danvers, I may very well return at some point in the future – the cruise ship stops here all the time, but I promise to do my best to stay out of trouble."

"Do you know how?" he shot back.

Schneider, Molly, and Pippin were close enough to hear our conversation, so too Sam and Gloria's Gang. They all looked at me to hear how I would respond, and their faces all bore version of the same expression: one which agreed with Captain Danvers.

I spurred my brain to deliver a witty comeback, but the back of my skull chose to itch, and a question formed instead.

"What happened to Shanice?"

The Accountant

"The cartel boss claimed they were not responsible for Chet Kowalski's murder," I reminded Captain Danvers.

Danny studied me, his head tilted slightly to the side while he waited to hear what I might say next.

There was a gap in the story. I started out believing Gloria's Gang had witnessed a murder. When we discovered Chet's death came at the end of a gun and not by strangulation, it changed things, but we continued to look for the same killer – the man with the mullet AKA Joey. He didn't do it either, which led me to the loan sharks, but they were in the clear out of basic principle – you don't kill a person who owes you money.

From there the next obvious choice became the Columbian Cartel though to be fair I didn't exactly work that out in advance, I stumbled upon the idea when we finally found William Chalice, the boss at Houston Investments.

However, Chet's death appeared to have nothing to do with the hedge fund company or what happened to them, and I believed Manolo Ravassa when he said his people were not behind it.

Pushing off the step, I rose to my feet. "I need to check on something. Have you taken the accountant away yet?"

Danny rose about halfway, so he was neither sitting nor standing, his eyes squinting when he looked down the street to the cop cars assembled inside the cordon.

"No, I don't think so. He caught a stray bullet in his left arm and was being treated last time I saw him. He's lucky to be alive and has already begged to give evidence against the cartel in return for a life in witness protection."

With my entourage trailing behind and Captain Danvers leading, I went in search of the man behind at least half the drama witnessed today. On the way, I remembered something and asked Jermaine for the data drive.

"What's this?" Danny asked.

"The log from the Roosevelt Building. I doubt you'll need it, but this should show the accountant was in the building like William claimed."

Danny pocketed the device as we got to the cartel's accountant.

Jakob Dershowitz was anything but Columbian.

"Sorry I tried to have you killed," he apologised before I could pose my first question.

Automatically, I wanted to say something like, 'That's okay', but stopped myself. Instead I said, "Why did you?"

I got a half shrug followed by a wince because shrugging hurt.

"Stay still," instructed the paramedic, a large black man who was not of a mind to tolerate a patient making his job harder.

Trying again, but without the movement, Jakob said, "I put a camera in the office last week. It was just in case, you know. I knew the Columbians wouldn't go to the police when I took their money, and I knew they would blame the staff at the hedge fund firm. The investment people would get tortured to death, but wouldn't be able to reveal what happened to the cartel's money because they would have no idea. Equally, the staff at Houston Investments couldn't go to the police because they were handling drug money.

It was the perfect scam – my retirement package. All I needed to do was lie low for a while, let things die down, and slip away unnoticed."

"Then you saw *me* in the office," I filled in the blank.

Jakob nodded his head, a sad smile and a faraway look on his face.

"Yeah. I panicked the previous day when the office was full of people. I thought they were FBI or something until I saw the cameras. Facial recognition software identified enough of them for me to know they were harmless, but when you showed up … well, I worried you might figure things out. I thought someone must have hired you to solve the case. They didn't though, did they?"

I didn't answer his question, I asked one of my own. I already knew the answer, but needed to hear his confirmation.

"Did you have Chet Kowalski killed?"

Jakob shifted his head to meet my eyes.

"No."

The Clues that got Missed

Captain Danvers was not happy about leaving the diabolical scene in Brooklyn, but was also kind of thankful to be able to hand over to someone else because the chief was on his way, and Danny was supposed to have gotten rid of me more than a day ago.

"Remind me again where we are going?" he asked.

We were back in his car, with two squad cars tailing behind, full to the brim with my friends. Because they started it all, Gloria, Peggy, and Pearl were on the backseat behind me, also curious to know what was going through my mind.

"I'll explain when we get there," I replied, giving a typically cryptic answer. Doing so reminded me of Barbie. I've done the same to her so many times and it drives her nuts that I won't explain my thoughts until the right moment arrives.

How was she getting on anyway? I hadn't heard from her in hours and that was unusual. Thinking she must be lost in her research and have no idea how many hours had ticked by, I took out my phone to call her.

When she didn't pick up, I took the phone away from my ear to check the signal strength. In the middle of a major city, I expected to have four bars and I did.

I tried again with the same result and sent her a message:

'It's been quite a day. Have solved the mystery of the missing money at Houston Investments and on my way to tie up the final loose end. Where are you? Everything okay?'

Glaring at the phone for the next thirty seconds, I dared it to ping back a response. None came. Sighing, I slipped the device back into its slot inside my handbag and looked up for the first time in more than a minute.

"Oh! This is it." With Captain Danvers at the wheel and his lights on to clear traffic from our path, we had crossed the city faster than anticipated.

"This place?" Captain Danvers angled into the kerb.

From the backseat, Gloria asked, "What are we doing back here?"

The answer to that question came down to one very simple fact: Linda Travers hadn't called the police when we left her place this morning. Checking dispatch had no logged calls from a person by that name took Captain Danvers less than thirty seconds.

It was the thing she was going to do next, and she chose not to. I would not have been able to figure out why had it not been for the elimination of suspects along the way. Making our way back up to her floor, I coached Captain Danvers on what I needed him to do.

"Are you serious?" he replied, struggling to believe my request.

"Anything else is likely to result in someone dying."

He looked doubtful, yet agreed to play along. For now.

So we wouldn't make too much noise, I asked everyone else to hang back near the elevators; we could not afford to spook Linda.

At her door, with Captain Danvers ready to knock and Jermaine standing over me like a protective shadow, I nodded that it was time to proceed.

Danny rapped his knuckles hard on the door.

"Debt collection," he barked, his gruff voice and local accent the only one in the group that wouldn't arouse suspicion.

Linda's voice echoed back, faint and muffled behind the door, yet still clear enough to hear when she said, "Just a minute."

I breathed a sigh of relief. That Linda would be at home was nothing more than a wild hunch on my part and I was pleased to have got that part right.

The locks on the inside slid back one after the other until the door began to open inward.

Linda got half a second to look surprised and then Captain Danvers was going through the door, forcing Chet's girlfriend back with his body as he advanced.

"Police," Captain Danvers announced, shoving his badge into her face. Raising his voice as he passed her, he shouted, "Police! Is there anyone here? Call out if you can hear me!"

"No!" cried Linda. "You're ruining it!"

Muffled voices came from deep within her apartment, their combined cries for help giving the game away.

Captain Danvers hurried, but as he ran through Linda's apartment, she reached behind her back to grab something tucked into the waistband of her jeans. There was not one shred of doubt in my mind that she was going for a gun and that was why I had Jermaine with me.

Fearing she might be armed, I was standing to one side so my faithful butler could close the distance and disarm her.

Her right arm got about halfway around her body, the barrel of the ugly, black automatic still pointing at the carpet when Jermaine's unyielding grip seized her wrist. His other hand ripped the gun from her grasp to a shocked cry of dismay.

She wailed again, "No! No, this is the only way! It's their fault, not mine!"

The muffled voices came clearer, Danny finding Linda's captives and removing their gags. With Gloria's Gang, four cops, Schneider and my team all coming down the hallway outside the apartment at speed, I went around Linda, confident she could do no more harm.

Bound with duct tape around their torsos, legs, and heads where the tape kept a sock stuffed inside their mouths, Shanice and Joey were struggling to get free. Captain Danvers tore at the tape with a pocketknife, cutting through to set Shanice loose.

Joey didn't have to wait his turn as two of the cops arrived in the bedroom while their captain still worked to remove the tape from Shanice's legs.

Finally loose from her bonds, Shanice threw herself at her boyfriend, hugging him tearfully now that their ordeal was over. This hampered the cops' attempts to remove the duct tape pinning his arms to his sides, but Joey didn't care.

"She was going to hand us over to a loan shark," he babbled. "She said it was our fault."

Shanice looked my way too. "She's completely nuts. She told me Chet borrowed money from some bad people and that they were holding Joey at her apartment. If I called the cops they would kill him, but when we got here, she pulled a gun on me."

My guess was slightly off the mark, but not by enough to make any difference.

Shanice was in a talkative mood and the crowd of people leaning through Linda's bedroom door or already inside the room were wont to listen.

"Joey wasn't here at all, but she didn't care about that. She seemed to think we had her money, or some money Chet borrowed or something. She went nuts when I said I had no idea what she was talking about. I thought she was going to kill me. She tied me up and gagged me, took the keys to my place, and left me here. I tried to call for help and I kept thumping the floor, but no one came," she sobbed through the last few words.

With Shanice unable to continue, Joey took over.

"I bumped into Linda outside the studio when I ran off to find Shanice. She told me the same story about loan sharks holding Shanice, but said she had the money that Chet borrowed and offered to let me have it so I could get Shanice back. When I got here, she hit me over the head. When I woke up, I was tied up and gagged next to Shanice."

Shanice managed to blurt, "She was going to hand us over to the loan sharks and tell them we had the money!"

The couple were free, and they were safe. They might need some trauma counselling, but otherwise, they would recover and there was nothing I could do for them.

Leaving the room, I found Linda in the kitchen. She was cuffed and sitting on a chair by a small table. Tears streamed down her face.

She looked up at my approach, her face filled with misery.

My question was a simple one to answer. "Did you mean to kill him?"

The words drew a sob that made her response hard to hear, but the shake of her head clarified it, "No."

Forced to wait until she calmed down and could speak again, I let Captain Danvers take over.

"Why don't you tell me what happened?"

Linda asked for a glass of water which a cop held to her lips so she could drink before she started talking.

Chet came to the city with a dream. He was going to be a famous actor, a face everyone knew. Of course, like so many others, his dream came to nothing, and Linda had to watch the mounting frustration as months turned into years and he moved from dead-end job to dead-end job, never really making ends meet.

Each time he went for an audition and got a call back, his hopes would soar because this was going to be the one. The depression that followed each time was hard for Linda to bear.

His latest idea to produce his own pilot for a TV show came after months of evening classes to learn screenplay writing, but Linda had no idea he was going to borrow money to do it. Worse yet, the money he borrowed from a loan shark when no bank would touch him, went in a flash and he stole Linda's savings to continue filming.

When she went to add a few more dollars to her pot of almost ten grand, only to discover it empty, she saw red. The gun was only to scare him into giving her back what was hers. She was dumping him; kicking him out and moving on with her life. There was a guy she liked at work and Linda knew he liked her back.

Lamenting that she should have kicked Chet to the kerb months earlier, she just needed her money back. But he didn't have it. Chet said it was almost all gone. Her savings had been blown on some stupid scheme that was never going to work and on top of that the idiot owed a loan shark ten thousand dollars and had no way to pay him back.

Even then, she didn't mean to shoot him. Chet went for the gun, and it went off; a single shot that tore through his heart and ended his life before his body hit the ground.

It was tragic. Two lives ruined for no good reason.

Captain Danvers sent her away between two uniformed officers and silence settled over those of us who were left.

"How did you know?" asked Pearl, the rest of those present leaning in to hear my response.

"It took me a while to figure it out," I admitted. "Really, it came down to a process of elimination and I remembered how Linda reacted this morning."

I got questioning looks from those who had been with me when we first visited her apartment.

"Gloria told her she saw Chet being killed." I reminded them. "Linda was horrified because she thought the ladies saw her shooting him."

"That's right," Peggy nodded her head. "She was so relieved when Gloria said we'd seen him being strangled. I didn't pick up on that."

"Neither did I," I replied. "Not until it was almost too late."

Joey and Shanice were given a clean bill of health by the paramedics and released by the police to go about their lives. They would provide full statements tomorrow or the next day.

Gloria's Gang were gone, so too Lieutenant Schneider with Sam. Molly and Pippin left to spend some time together in the city. That left just me and Jermaine.

The cops were clearing out and there was no reason for me to still be sitting on the couch in Linda and Chet's apartment other than I felt completely bushed. I kept willing my feet to get moving, but they stayed where they were until my phone rang.

Assuming it was Barbie finally returning my call, I was just as pleased to see Alistair's name on my phone. There was nothing more he could do to get the ship fixed and wanted to spend some time with me.

It was an invitation to dinner and a promise to take me somewhere swanky. Feeling my energy levels renewed, I found Danny in the hallway outside the apartment where he was talking to the chief of police.

The chief eyed me like he'd just trodden in something unpleasant.

Shifting his gaze to glare at Captain Danvers, he growled, "You were supposed to send her back to her ship."

Danvers winked at me with the eye on the opposite side to his boss, the senior man missing the gesture.

"I tried," Danny shrugged.

"Well try harder, man," the chief barked. "She's a menace."

"She's standing right in front of you," I pointed out, unhappy at how blatantly rude he chose to be.

Focusing his surly demeanour on me, he grumbled, "I understand you continued to pursue the case you were instructed to leave alone," he grumbled unhappily.

Had he been in a position to do anything about it, I felt certain he would be acting already, but what could he say or do? With my team, through luck or persistence, we had solved several crimes, saved two people, and removed the Columbian Cartel from the city.

"That's right," I replied happily. My response was not the one he expected and caught off guard by my unrepentant attitude he floundered.

"Well ... Well." He could start a sentence, but found himself lost immediately thereafter.

"Don't worry, sir," Captain Danvers used his right arm to move me along down the hallway, Jermaine, as always, in my shadow, "I'll make sure Mrs Fisher returns to her ship without causing any more bother."

Six paces later, when we were tangibly out of the chief's earshot, Danny whispered, "You won't cause any more trouble, will you?"

I looked his way and shrugged with a big, wide grin.

"I promise I won't mean to."

Where's Barbie

Jermaine stayed with me until we met with Alistair. Certain I would need a change of outfit for whatever high-end eatery he was taking me to – my clothes were still on me, but stained and dirty from the trials of the day – I could only laugh when he pushed open the door of a deli.

"What?" he offered a mock confused face. "This place serves the best sandwiches in town."

I was about hungry enough to eat a scabby horse, but his claim proved accurate. Hot slices of pastrami between thick cut bread served with mild mustard and sides of spicy pickles and giant French fries satisfied my needs on numerous levels. The portions were so generous I couldn't finish mine, yet I still felt robbed when Alistair gobbled down the final few fries from my plate.

Basking in the glow of a fine meal with the person I love, I knew happiness and satisfaction. Alistair held my hand across the table and looked into my eyes. We didn't need to say words; spending time with each other was enough.

My phone rang again, and this time I knew it had to be Barbie.

I was wrong yet again: it was Hideki.

Thumbing the green button I tucked the phone under my hair where I pressed it to my left ear.

"Hideki? Is everything all right?"

"Have you heard from Barbie?" he asked, no preliminary conversation needed.

Worry shot through me like an icy spear to my heart.

"No. Not for hours. She left me to head to the museum."

I heard Hideki exhale through his nose, a sound of frustration.

"No one knows where she is." Hideki's words made me sit upright, my grip on Alistair's hand tightening with my fear. "She's not at the museum and there is no record of her going through the turnstile today."

Thinking fast, I said, "She was meeting someone. Um, a junior curator of some kind."

"Yes. His name is Hugo Lockhart. I met him yesterday. No one knows where he is either."

I rose to my feet, letting go of Alistair's hand and checking to make sure I had all my things because we were leaving.

"Where are you now?" I asked.

"At the museum." I could hear the worry in Hideki's voice. It didn't belong there; he wasn't the kind of person who got rattled. "The whole team is here. They came the moment I alerted them. Something's not right, Patricia."

Flashing my eyes at Alistair – he was hearing enough of my half of the conversation to know what was going on, I said, "I'm on my way. Don't worry. I'm sure she's just locked in a research room somewhere lost in a book."

They were words of hopeful encouragement, but I didn't believe them. Barbie was missing and it had something to do with the San José. That could only mean one thing.

Epilogue

- -

B arbie twisted in place as she tried to get comfortable. The plastic binds pinning her wrists together pinched her skin and were going to leave deep bruises. The wounds were insignificant though; she was more worried about where she was going.

Convinced she was onto something, she'd spent more than four hours reading through the diary of Casa Alegre, the captain of the San José. What was instantly clear was that the Spanish treasure ship evaded the British in 1708 – his diary entries continued after the date on which the ship was supposed to have gone to the bottom.

Hugo Lockhart had been beside himself with excitement, ranting about how this would prove to be the greatest maritime discovery of the century. Barbie couldn't understand why he wasn't involving his colleagues; surely they would be just as excited.

Thinking back, Barbie recognised that his behaviour was a clue she should have noticed. However, she'd been too engrossed at the time to give it much thought.

He kept asking her questions, wanting to know how she had been so sure the San José wasn't sunk by the British as the history books claim. Did she know something she was choosing to keep secret? Had she uncovered evidence no one else knew about?

Inevitably, despite the fascinating subject matter, her bodily functions demanded she visit the ladies' restroom. Escorted by Hugo, she followed him from their private research room along a corridor and past a restroom that claimed to be out of order.

"There's another just through here," he assured her, just a little bit too keen to make sure she got to the right place.

Again, his behaviour was off, but she only recognised it afterwards when it was too late.

Passing through a door that to her looked to be leading them outside, she shrieked when a giant arm snaked around her shoulders the moment she stepped into the daylight. Hugo's deception had taken her into a loading bay behind the museum.

Her startled cry lasted less than a second, shut off when a hand the size of a dinner plate closed over her mouth and nose.

Unable to breath, but fighting for all she was worth, unconsciousness came in less than a minute.

When she came to it was dark, the lack of light disorienting. Messages flooded in from all over her body in the moments that followed: she was tied up, she was on a plane, and she had been drugged.

The grogginess of whatever they'd given her was wearing off, but fighting against her bonds quickly proved futile. Besides, if she was on a plane, where would she go even if she was able to get her limbs free?

The biggest and most concerning question in her mind was a very simple one: Where am I going?

The End

Author's Note:

H ello, Dear Reader,

It is the middle of the afternoon on a Wednesday in May and the sun is blazing down outside to give us the first properly warm day of the year. Ironically, I sold my convertible sports car about two hours ago.

I bought it on a whim almost two years ago and have barely driven it since. I didn't own a car for more than two years after moving to be a full-time author, and convinced myself it was okay to spend a little of my money on something fun.

And it was fun. Especially for my son, Hunter, who was five when daddy arrived home in the sleek, black Mercedes.

It was also completely impractical, and I very soon realised I was going to want to put both children into my car at some point. That wasn't going to work with a two-seater. Now I have an offroad thing that is old enough to go to university and will be an excellent workhorse for many years. I hope.

This book has taken me longer to write than any in the last three years. Not because I struggled to understand the story, or found myself suffering writer's block (what the heck is that anyway?). No, I struggled because I have so many other projects all going on at the same time.

Naively, I took on assistants thinking they would take work off my plate and I would be able to focus on crafting tales. I feel, quite often, that the opposite is true. They perform tasks I don't have time for, and for the most part these were tasks I wasn't doing in the first place. Worse yet, I have to learn the tasks I never found time for so I can hand them over to someone else. Then I have to check they are doing them right.

I am absolutely not moaning even though that is exactly what it sounds like.

In this story I refer to Commander Schooner. He first appeared all the way back in the first Patricia Fisher story 'The Missing Sapphire of Zangrabar'. I can say no more than that for fear you may be reading this as your first Patricia Fisher book and to say more would ruin things.

Let's just say he and Patricia did not get along and leave it at that. If you want to know more, grab book one and indulge yourself in Patricia's origin story.

I knew the Aurelia was going to be in New York for this book, but with endless options for what the story could be, I almost wrote a sideways take on the *Bruce Willis* film, *Die Hard*. I might yet write that tale at some point just because I want Patricia to say, 'Yippee Ki Yay, dear," to a terrorist before something terrible happens to them.

I'm not one for giving the readers cliff-hangers. I find them annoying as a reader unless you are able to power straight into the next book. I will, however, reveal that many of my contemporaries swear by them. There is no better way to lead your readers into the next book than by leaving them with a tantalising open hook.

Well, there is a cliff hanger of sorts in this story, but I won't make people wait to find out what happens. I have a whole list of books I need to write, but will be powering straight into the next story in this series right after I craft a new something with Albert and Rex.

What's that? Who are Albert and Rex?

That's a question you can easily answer via my website for which there are links below, or by jumping over to Amazon. Albert and Rex are my best selling series; tales of mayhem and mystery with a curmudgeonly old, retired police detective and his sidekick, an over-sized German Shepherd.

Their adventures are about to enter a second series, but I have one or two more short stories to tell just to round out their trip around the British Isles.

Anyway, I think that's enough teasing for now.

I hope you enjoyed this book.

Take care.

Steve Higgs

What's next for Patricia?

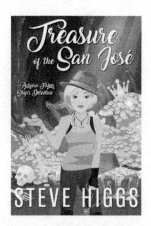

More than three hundred years ago, the officers and crew of a Spanish treasure ship embarked on a quest to pull off the greatest heist the world would ever know.

What became of them has remained hidden by time, but now two parties are closing in on the truth and the billions in gold and jewels that went missing all those years ago.

Xavier Silvestre wants the treasure. He is rich, resourceful, and ruthless. He also has one of Patricia Fisher's friends and that's more than enough to get her involved.

Patricia has no interest in the treasure, she just wants her gang to feel whole again, but she doesn't know who the other treasure hunter is, and she has no idea where he is. The only thing she does know is what he wants, and she plans to find it first.

Get ready for white-knuckle adventure.

Free Books and More

Want to see what else I have written? Go to my website.

https://stevehiggsbooks.com/

Or sign up to my newsletter where you will get sneak peaks, exclusive giveaways, behind the scenes content, and more. Plus, you'll be notified of Fan Pricing events when they occur and get exclusive offers from other authors because all UF writers are automatically friends.

Copy the link into your web browser.

https://stevehiggsbooks.com/newsletter/

Prefer social media? Join my thriving Facebook community.

Want to join the inner circle where you can keep up to date with everything? This is a free group on Facebook where you can hang out with likeminded individuals and enjoy discussing my books. There is cake too (but only if you bring it).

https://www.facebook.com/groups/1151907108277718

About the Author

At school, the author was mostly disinterested in every subject except creative writing, for which, at age ten, he won his first award. However, calling it his first award suggests that there have been more, which there have not. Accolades may come but, in the meantime, he is having a ball writing mystery stories and crime thrillers and claims to have more than a hundred books forming an unruly queue in his head as they clamour to get out. He lives in the south-east corner of England with a duo of lazy sausage dogs. Surrounded by rolling hills, brooding castles, and vineyards, he doubts he will ever leave, the beer is just too good.

Printed in Great Britain
by Amazon

38913603R00109